A MESSAGE FROM CHICKEN HOUSE

I used to have a magic kit. I would practise for hours, trying out tricks that had the power to amaze and baffle – if I ever got good enough. Of course, I believed that was the only kind of magic in existence – but what if it wasn't? What if I could have found out about a different kind of magic . . . *real* magic?

That's exactly what happens for our main character, Alex, who loves tricks even more than I did. Strange forces are at play, old enmities stirred and an unforgettable friendship forged . . . and yes, the secrets of *real* magic are so much more thrilling, touching and extraordinary than I could ever have imagined! Clever Guy Jones reveals all – or does he?

BARRY CUNNINGHAM
Publisher
Chicken House

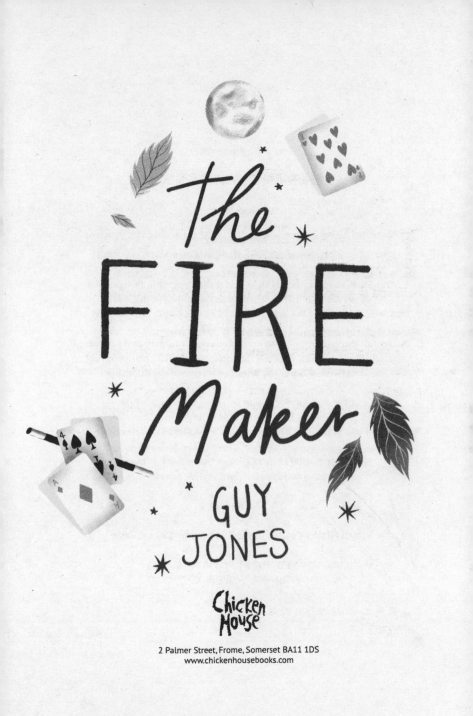

The FIRE Maker

GUY JONES

Chicken House

2 Palmer Street, Frome, Somerset BA11 1DS
www.chickenhousebooks.com

Text © Guy Jones 2019

First published in Great Britain in 2019
Chicken House
2 Palmer Street
Frome, Somerset BA11 1DS
United Kingdom
www.chickenhousebooks.com

Cover and interior design by Helen Crawford-White
Typeset by Dorchester Typesetting Group Ltd
Printed and bound in Great Britain by CPI Group (UK) Ltd, Croydon CR0 4YY

The paper used in this Chicken House book is made
from wood grown in sustainable forests.

1 3 5 7 9 10 8 6 4 2

British Library Cataloguing in Publication data available.

PB ISBN 978-1-911490-67-8
eISBN 978-1-912626-13-7

For Mum and Dad

Also by Guy Jones

The Ice Garden

Alex charged down the alley and into The Wick. Shouts rang out behind; savage and hoarse. A metallic tang of blood in the back of his nose and throat.

When he was younger, this place – a broad patch of woodland tucked away amongst the houses – had been Alex's whole world. His playground. It was pristine jungle he'd been the first to discover. A faraway forest planet on which humans were building a new home. The lair of lions and tigers and dinosaurs, and awful things that didn't have names because nobody who'd seen one had ever lived to tell the tale. And, often, it had been a war zone, with Alex outwitting imaginary enemy soldiers.

Not so imaginary now, though. The sound of snapping branches and cursing rang behind him.

Days of rain had made the ground slick, but Alex kept his balance, avoiding the patches of sucking mud. He could only hope his classmates weren't so deft. Branches clawed at him, thorn bushes snagged and tore his clothes. Yet the noises were getting further away. Perhaps he was losing them . . .

He sprinted into a small clearing. At its centre was a single, huge tree. It was a strange old thing, with a stocky, S-shaped trunk from which four huge branches emerged like the fingers of a gnarled hand. Thick green moss coated the lower reaches, but the bark itself was black, as if blasted by lightning: burnt and hardened into jet.

Alex didn't pause, sprinting across the open ground and into the bushes on the far side. Soon, another line of boundary fencing loomed up. He'd run into a dead end, it seemed. But Alex knew this place. Knew the secret ways in and out. He fell to his knees and ran his hand across the bottom of the fence; desperately hoping no one had done a repair job in the past year or two. His heart skipped. There it was!

He levered the loose panel aside, creating a hole to the road on the other side. He had to wriggle through, leaving his uniform caked in mud and slime. For a moment Alex worried what his father would say, before remembering how ridiculous that was.

Once he was through, he set about replacing the panel. His pursuers would make their way to the fence and think he'd vanished into thin air. How was that for a magic trick? Job done, he turned his face to the darkening September sky. Fat raindrops began to fall.

A laugh. It came from beside him. Instantly Alex realized his mistake. Because he hadn't played alone in The Wick all those times. It wasn't only him who'd learnt the secret ways in and out. He'd done it all with his best friend. Now former best friend. He turned to find Freddie Taylor standing there, grinning.

'Thought I'd forgotten?' Freddie said, stepping forward. Alex could hear the other two blundering around on the other side but paid them barely any mind.

It was such a familiar face – pale skin spattered with freckles, and flaming hair that tumbled towards green-blue eyes. A kind face. Or at least it had been. Now all the light was gone, shrouded by fury.

'You know what she's going to say,' his ex-friend hissed, so close that Alex felt wet drops of spittle on his face.

He didn't need to be told who 'she' was. Freddie's mother, Agnes Taylor. A huge woman with a volcanic temper. Alex almost felt bad, but what was he meant to have done? He'd kept silent since February; ever since the Incident. He'd said nothing as Freddie and pals had made fun of him. As they pushed him or elbowed him in the ribs. He was silent when they threw his books away or got him in trouble with the teachers. In short, he'd sucked up every last bit of punishment they'd thrown his way. There were nights that he'd turned his pillow wet with tears of frustration, but never once had he told.

Until today. Today had been too much. He'd told on Freddie, who had been sent straight to the Deputy Head.

And now, this would be revenge.

'He's here!' Freddie shouted, grabbing hold of Alex's blazer so roughly the buttons were pulled loose. 'Come through the fence.'

The sound of scrabbling from the other side. Alex felt his skin run with electricity. But then something disturbed a cat, which leapt down from the fence with a yowl. Freddie's head turned for a second, which was all the invitation Alex needed.

He wrenched free and barrelled past and into the night. The roads blurred around him. Street lamps were reflected and warped by the soaking tarmac. He jagged this way and that through the town centre and into the houses beyond. The streets were narrow here and choked with parked cars. Lights blazed in the windows, and televisions flickered. Alex passed it all like a ghost on the wind, running so smoothly he was almost flowing. But all the time his pursuer's feet splashed along behind.

At last he could run no more and stumbled to a halt, gasping. Stars burst in front of his eyes. How could Freddie still be chasing? How could they *still* be coming after him? Was this how it would always be now? Was this his life? Running, hiding, looking over his shoulder . . . He blinked back the tears pooling in his eyes.

What now; what next? Alex scanned around and found a garden gate in the middle of a tall fence. He lurched across the road and tried the handle, almost punching the air in relief as it turned. He slipped inside, closed it behind him and pressed his ear to the wood. His head filled with the smell of old timber and creosote. A memory came, unbidden, of helping his dad stain their garden fence a few summers before, carefully applying the sticky brown liquid to each panel in turn.

Footsteps approached, passed, and receded into the distance. Alex slumped to the ground, coughing. Safe. For a little while at least, he was safe.

He opened his eyes and pulled himself up. And that was when he saw them.

That was when he saw something extraordinary.

2

Alex gaped.

He was in a perfectly normal-looking garden, with a crooked old apple tree and a shed off to one side. The grass was blue-grey in the moonlight and there were lights on in the upstairs window of the house. But there was something else too. Something so strange that he could do nothing but stare, open-mouthed. Something that, for a few seconds, his mind refused to believe could really be there . . .

Three orange lights hovered above the lawn. Each was about the size of a small egg, and they hung in the air, bobbing gently up and down. Alex pulled himself to his feet and the orbs darted away from him, as if afraid. He hardly dared breathe.

Looking closer he realized the lights weren't glowing so much as burning. They flickered and flared like candles. Inside each one was a small, darker shape from which the fire seemed to come.

'What are you?' he whispered. The fireballs responded to his voice by starting to move, sketching slow lines of flame in the darkness. Round and round they went, as if in some strange ballet, their movements all grace and ease. Alex could do nothing but gawp.

The three of them circled for a while, at times coming so close he could feel their warmth. The air was laced with the scent of hot sand and baking rocks – rich and heady. He turned to follow them as they skimmed low over the grass, tracing patterns of light that hung in the air for a moment, as if a child had been writing with a sparkler. Every now and then he could have sworn he heard one of them make a sound; almost like a tinkling laugh of delight.

He didn't know how long he watched. Moonlight crept across the lawn. The clouds broke above. Alex could see their torn edges; stars peeking out from the gaps in-between. Eventually though, one of the lights came nearer and paused there, as if considering him. He could hear the blood pounding in his ears.

It was hypnotic; like staring into the depths of a log fire. The flames danced in yellow, black and orange. As Alex watched, a wave of dizziness came over him, not sickly but pleasant. He felt calm, almost woozy, as if he were falling slowly through a night sky consumed with flames that only warmed and did no harm. The firestorm was all around and deep within him too.

Alex reached out with his thoughts.

How was that even possible?

His mind was reacting in a way he didn't understand and could barely even control. It flowed towards the thing as if wanting to brush fingers with it. As if wanting to start to build trust between them. The creature – if that's what it was – sent waves of gentle heat back towards him. They flowed through every cell of his body; a sensation both comforting and dangerous.

What's happening to me? The shout came from another part of his mind – the part that needed to understand the world in black and white. Alex panicked and felt his own fear run along the connection between them like an electric shock. The thing leapt and scooted back into the corner of the garden like a frightened cat.

His head swam, as if he'd stood up too quickly from a hot bath. Both legs went from under him and he fell, knocking over a tall terracotta pot as he went. It hit the ground with a loud crash, smashing into pieces on the paving slabs. The creatures responded with a flurry of movement, zipping back and forth in agitation.

Alex pulled himself up on to all fours, shaking his head clear of the fog inside.

A light came on at the back of the house. *Someone*

heard! Someone was coming.

With one last glance at the buzzing balls of flame, Alex picked himself up, squeezed out through the gate, and sprinted for home.

3

Alex punched in the combination and the gate swung open. The house was modern but handsome, with large windows along the ground and first floor, and a few smaller ones peeking out from the sloped roof. The grounds were immaculate despite the rain, and the smell of wet grass was full and round in his nose. There was no car in the drive and no lights on inside. His dad's promise to be back early had obviously hit a bump in the road. He had a sudden, violent longing for the whole place to go to rack and ruin; for the ivy to run wild and choke the walls until they crumbled; for the whole town of Hatford Cross to be swallowed up by the earth.

He closed the front door behind him and let out a

juddering sigh. What on earth had been in that garden? He could still feel the creatures' presence in his mind. No, not *presence*. More like an imprint. A residue, but fading fast, like soap bubbles left in the sink.

He examined his reflection in the mirror on the opposite wall. Hair plastered to his forehead and peppered with tiny, pearl-like raindrops. Eyes red, as if he'd been crying without realizing. He made his way to the downstairs bathroom and splashed cold water on his face. It sent chills right down to the soles of his feet.

He paused for a moment by the photo of a much younger him being hoisted into the air by his dad. There were gaps in his smile where baby teeth had fallen out and new ones hadn't yet grown through. They were both dressed in shorts and T-shirts, their faces cracked open by laughter. The picture was crooked, but Alex didn't bother to straighten it on his way out.

An iron radiator ran the length of the hall towards the kitchen at the back. Visitors – mostly his dad's work friends these days – would often comment on it, and his father would look sheepish and mutter something that let them know how expensive it had been without looking like he was boasting. Alex just thought it ugly. It was on now, and the air reeked of scorched dust.

There was no sound but his own breathing. The silence was so huge that it seemed almost like a house guest, and an unwelcome one at that. Alex swept up a remote control and switched on the television in the lounge. The programme was trash, but it was a relief to hear friendly voices. One of his blazer buttons had come loose where Freddie had grabbed him. He took the sewing tin from the cupboard and set about repairing the damage.

After that he prepared dinner. The knife flashed and danced as it carved the wooden board. Close-up magic was good practice for cookery; it made your hands strong and precise. Into the pan went the ingredients and soon the kitchen was redolent with the sweet, sharp smell of onions and garlic. Alex ate lounging on the sofa with the plate on his lap. The TV chattered away but his mind was dragged back time and again to the events of that lunchtime.

He'd been in the form room, practising with his favourite deck of cards. They were old and worn: a present from his parents when he had first told them he wanted to learn magic. He'd been so engrossed in what he was doing he hadn't heard Freddie and two other goons creep up behind him. The first he'd known about them was when the deck was snatched from his hand.

'What should I do with these then?' Freddie had said.

'How about just giving them back?' he'd snapped.

'Or how about this?' Freddie had plucked a card from the deck and ripped it in two.

Alex tried to protest but only a strangled wheeze

emerged. The next card went the same way and then the next and the next. By the end, the two boys hadn't needed to hold him still – all the life had drained from him. The deck of cards he'd treasured for five years was scattered across the floor like confetti.

You never tell. That's the rule. The teachers, the parents; they don't need to know. Yet he *had* told, and now things were even worse.

Alex flicked the TV off and went to his room. The walls were plastered with vintage posters of old magicians like Houdini, Carter the Great and Harry Blackstone. The illustrations were insane riots of imagination, filled with fork-tailed demons and flowing robes. Just looking at them made Alex's heart tap out a quicker beat. There were playing cards, wands and chains; all hinting at the wonders the audience might see. And always there was the magician himself – immaculate in his tuxedo and bow tie, controlling the forces around him.

There were images of modern performers too, and in pride of place was Alex's signed picture of Jack Kellar. It didn't seem to matter if it was close-up magic or grand illusions – Kellar was a master. Alex sat at his desk and pulled a dog-eared envelope from the drawer. It had arrived at the start of the summer and by now the paper was grubby from so much handling. He took out the letter and smoothed it on the desk.

Dear Alex,

Thank you for your interest in Young Magician of the Year. We enjoyed watching your audition tape and think you show huge potential. It is therefore with great pleasure that we would like to invite you to attend the London and South-East heats where you will join fourteen more up-and-coming magicians, all hoping to make the national finals.

The competition will take place on Saturday 29 September and you are asked to prepare a performance lasting for five minutes. We know you will be excited to learn that this year's Guest Judge is none other than world-renowned illusionist, Jack Kellar.

Congratulations on making it to this stage of the competition, and we look forward to seeing the wonders you can conjure.

James H. W. Donaldson

General Secretary

The Magic Society

Alex could still hardly believe it. In just over a week he'd not only be competing against the best young magicians in the region; he'd be doing it in front of Jack Kellar!

With the letter stowed safely back in the drawer he stood up and closed his eyes. If he tried hard he could push away his surroundings and imagine instead that he was in the wings of a theatre. In front of him was a stage and there, just out of sight for the time being, the audience. He stepped out and heard the ripple of applause as he took his place under the hot lights.

Alex ran through his routine. He vanished coins into thin air and made them appear again. He had no one to pick-a-card-any-card for him, but he went through the motions anyway, playing both parts, making sure his movements were accurate and smooth. He displayed a blank sheet of paper which a moment later was filled with writing, and a full box of cards, which emptied with a click of his fingers. For the finale, he tore a signed banknote to shreds only to find it reassembled in his jacket pocket.

He stopped. Sweat pooled at his throat. The audience inside his mind was silent. It wasn't good enough. It was solid, sure, but nothing that a thousand magicians hadn't done a thousand times before. Ordinary people might be impressed, but Jack Kellar was no ordinary person. Alex kicked out at his bedpost in frustration. *He wasn't good enough.* The competition was in a week!

His phone buzzed and he glanced down at the screen. It seemed his father would have to work late this Friday evening after all.

4

A market on a city street. People drift by in clumps. In the background are stalls crammed with knick-knacks. The shot tracks to a man. He's in a suit, but he wears it more like a movie star than a business-man. He's tall and slim, with dark skin and thinning hair arranged to look perfectly untidy. With him is a group of teenage guys and girls, who are giggling and making faces into the camera. The man watches them with a small smile on his face, and then asks for their attention, which they give to him instantly.

One of the boys is wearing a hoodie. The man asks if it's new and the boy says it is. The man asks if it's expensive and the boy confirms that too. The man asks if the boy would mind him trying it on, and the group *erupts in laughter.*

The man laughs along for a few seconds but then asks the question again. Once more the group falls in line. It's almost as if he has them on a leash, letting them run and then pulling them back at will. The boy shrugs and hands him the top. The man drapes his own suit jacket around the boy's shoulders to keep him warm and the gang starts to giggle again.

The man puts a hand on the boy's shoulder and looks straight at him. The kid glances to his friends, all at once feeling a little unsure. 'I want to try something,' says the man. 'Do you trust me?'

More laughter, but nervous this time. A sense of threat has appeared, as if from nowhere.

The boy gives his permission and the man produces a metal rubbish bin into which he throws the hoodie. Then, lightning fast and before anyone can object, he strikes three matches and sends them into the can. Flames erupt in an instant, and the camera zooms in first on the burning hoodie and then on the open-mouthed face of its owner. The boy's eyes are popping from his head, but he's too shocked to protest.

The man waits a few more seconds then takes a bottle of water from one of the group and uses it to douse the fire. The camera goes in for a closer look, revealing a charred, soggy mess. Then it pulls up to the man who is, for the first time, looking worried. He holds his hands up. 'Look, guys, um . . .' he says. 'That was . . . I mean, that wasn't meant to go quite like that.'

'That was new! My wallet was in there!' the boy shouts, and the man backs off a couple of paces.

'OK, OK. I'll replace it obviously. What shop did you get it from?'

The boy tells him.

'No problem, I can go there. And your wallet too, I'll replace that too. I've got some money in my bag. Look, it's just there. Can someone . . . ?'

The group turn and see a black rucksack leaning against a market stall just behind them. They glance at one another. One of the girls goes to get it.

'Just inside,' says the man.

The girl unzips the bag and pulls something out. It's a hoodie. She unfolds it. It's identical to the one that was just burnt. The boy grabs it from his friend.

'Look in the pocket,' the man tells him, and the boy draws out his wallet. 'That's yours, right?' he asks. 'That's it, right?'

The group goes bananas.

The man has that little smile on his face again. 'I'll have my jacket back,' he says, and ruffles the kid's hair.

The screen fades to a swirling darkness, from the midst of which two words emerge, etched in silver . . . Jack Kellar.

5

The next morning Alex came downstairs to find his dad tucking into an enormous sausage sandwich. And, joy! A couple left in the pan for him. He tucked them between two slices of bread with a thick layer of brown sauce.

As he took a seat at the breakfast bar his dad glanced up from his phone. 'Sorry I was late last night,' he said.

'That's all right.'

'Work, you know?'

Alex did. Only too well.

'Do I look tired to you, Al?'

There was a time Alex would have reacted to this, but he'd told his father a thousand times how much he hated his name being shortened and it did no good.

Instead, he took the opportunity to look. In truth, his dad *did* look tired. He was a handsome man, with thick, greying hair and tanned skin. But there were dark moons hanging under his eyes, and the flesh on his face seemed softer than Alex remembered. Strange, he thought, that if you really *stared* at someone, they could all of a sudden seem less familiar. It was like repeating a word over and over until it became nothing more than a meaningless sound.

'You look good,' he lied.

His dad flashed a smile. Genuine, warm.

'What time do you want to go?' Alex asked.

'Go?'

Cold fingers gripped at his heart. Disappointment so sharp he could taste it. 'You said we'd go and get me a suit,' he said. Work emails shone from his dad's phone, calling for his attention. 'For the *Young Magician* heats next weekend,' Alex pressed on. 'You said you'd get me a suit to wear.'

Alex's dad tipped his head back and groaned. 'God, I did, didn't I?'

'We only need to go to one shop, Dad. I know what I'm looking for.'

'I know; but just what with getting into town, finding a parking space and queuing and all . . .'

'It's still early. Won't be too busy.' Alex kept his voice bright, but the final threads of hope were fast coming loose.

'You know what the town centre's like on a Saturday, Al.'

Alex nodded. Four-by-fours choking streets made originally for horse and carts. But still . . .

'And you can't just wear your normal clothes?'

'Dad, I'll be on stage.'

'You've got smart stuff up there in the wardrobe.'

It's Young Magician of the Year, Alex thought. *Jack Kellar will be there. It has to be perfect.* But he stayed quiet.

'Look,' his dad said, crossing to one of the kitchen cupboards. 'You know what work's like at the moment. I've got a pile of stuff to get through today.'

'It's Saturday,' Alex muttered.

'Exactly. Imagine how I feel.' Alex's dad turned back towards him and extended his hand. 'This should be enough,' he said.

Alex looked. A wad of banknotes. His skin prickled and crawled. *You said you'd come with me*, he wanted to shout. *You said you'd help me pick. You said we'd do it together.*

'That should be enough, shouldn't it?' his dad asked. 'You'll be able to get yourself a cracking suit with that. I know how important this is to you.'

Alex forced himself to nod and smile. 'Thank you,' he managed. 'That's really generous.'

His dad messed his hair with one hand while reaching for his emails again with the other.

Alex stared at the phone: sleek black and glowing white. He pictured the inside of it – the circuits and chips and all the rest – everything that made it what it was. If only it would break. No, not break. If only it would burst into flame and melt, right there on the table. What would his dad do then? Alex willed it. He summoned every ounce of mental energy that he could and directed it straight into the device. He told the plastic to buckle, the screen to crack, the silicon to bubble with impossible heat. He willed it to shrivel and burn away to nothing.

But, of course, nothing happened. There was no such thing as real magic, and boys couldn't melt phones with their minds.

His father glanced up for a half second, as if surprised that Alex was still there.

'I'll get going then, Dad,' he said.

'Have a good time,' came the reply. But the words were vacant. As empty and weightless as space.

6

Alex kept a careful eye out as he trudged the twenty minutes or so into the centre of Hatford Cross. Chances were that Agnes Taylor had Freddie safely locked down after the previous day's call home from school, but the two goons could be lurking somewhere. They'd be more than happy to land a kick or two if it meant getting some brownie points from their leader.

James Gilfoy and Samuel Down. Not the usual bullying types at all. Both of them were good in class, and neither was the slow, hulking monster that you might expect. And yet both were now committed to the idea of making Alex's life a living nightmare. That was Freddie for you – magnetic, somehow. Alex had known it himself when they were friends – that feeling that you wanted to please this person if you possibly could. That you'd do anything to avoid letting them down. And ever since the Incident, that same power had gone to work turning the school against him.

The rain had cleared, and the streets were bathed in a milky sort of sunshine. A few leaves lay red-gold in the gutter like shards of tarnished copper.

It was market day. Stalls sprawled along the high street, selling everything from fruit and veg to foam mattresses, farmhouse cheeses to knock-off designer jeans. The traders' cries rang out, harsh and clear.

'Lovely peppers, pound a bowl!'

'Flowers! Going quick! How about you, young man? Get some for your mum? She'll thank you for it!'

Alex struggled on through the stream of people. Dogs trotted at their owners' feet. Black crows perched on the telephone wires overhead. Huge silver-grey bins gaped ready to receive the cast-offs of the day – the broken, the spoilt, the merely unwanted.

A couple of girls from his year at school swept towards him, carried on the tide and laughing high-pitched peals. Alex raised a hand in greeting, but they went past without seeing him.

His mind turned to the suit he wanted. Plain black jacket and trousers, with a narrow tie, which he would wear with a white shirt – top button undone. It would be a simple, classic look. The kind of thing that mixed old-time sophistication with a touch of modern cool. Alex had watched videos of the previous year's contestants. You wouldn't believe some of them! Eleven-year-olds in full tuxedos and bow ties. Or enormous velvet jackets they'd found at the back of some wardrobe somewhere. Not for him, though. He was going to look the part. Just like Jack Kellar.

The shouting came from the post office.

Alex paused as he passed the door and cast a look across the road to the suit shop. His perfect outfit could wait a few minutes more, he thought, so he ducked inside to see what was happening.

'You're all crooks! Crooks and robbers!'

There was an old man at the counter. Side on, Alex could see a shock of wire-wool hair sat atop craggy features framed by a scratchy-looking beard. He was small and spry-looking inside a baggy suit. A plastic screen sat between him and the lady serving, which was a good job given the volume and fury of the man's complaint. With every utterance he would fling his arms back and forth, as if conducting an orchestra or hurling his words at their unfortunate recipient.

'Sir, if you could listen to me for a second,' tried the young woman behind the counter gamely. Alex thought he recognized her from his school's sixth form.

'Listen to you?' the man shot back instantly. 'Listen to you?! Why would I listen to you? Why would I listen to your lies? Why would I listen to your lying, snaking words? You lie as easily as water pours downhill. You lie as easily as milk goes off in the sun. You lie as easily as I turn the page of a book.'

He mimed turning the page, and Alex had to admit it did look quite easy.

'Why would I listen when all I get is lies? Don't you think I know what's going on here? Don't you think I know what you people are trying to pull?!'

The girl wasn't given a chance to respond.

'Well, I do!' the man went on. 'I know your game, post-office serving lady. I know that you may look all nice and sweet and whatnot, but I know you're a thief. You and all your post-office friends. Thieves and rotten eggs!'

A long line of people waited behind the man. Usually, Alex thought, they would have grumbled and tutted at the delay. But instead they were entranced – staring with open mouths and wide eyes at the extraordinary performance in front of them. The man was to making a fuss what Da Vinci was to painting, or Houdini to magic.

Now the man sucked in a deep breath and seemed about to explode into another rant, when a woman stepped out of a door marked *Private – Staff Only*. She had shoulder-length, greying hair and eyes that had seen far too much complaining for one lifetime.

'Hello, Mr Olmos,' she said, with bone-deep weariness.

'Ah-ha!' the man exclaimed in triumph. 'I wondered how long it would take you to show your face, Mrs Manager.'

'Would you like to step to one side?'

'No, I would not! I would like to stay exactly where I am, until I get some answers.'

'If you step aside then other people can be served.'

'Served?! You call this service? Your young woman here . . .' At that, he turned and peered at the badge of the girl behind the counter.

'Rose,' she offered.

'Rose!' Mr Olmos agreed. 'Rose here doesn't know the meaning of the word *served*. She is deliberately trying to frustrate me.'

'Mr Olmos, we go through this every week. Why don't you tell me what the problem is this time?'

'The problem? Oh, I'll tell you what the problem is!'

The watching crowd took in a collective breath. Alex thought they'd only be happier if they had some popcorn in hand.

'I ordered an item,' he declared with utmost seriousness.

'An item. I see,' replied the manager.

'An item that should have arrived in the post. I received a card through my door saying that they had tried to deliver it, but that I wasn't at home.'

'We've been through this before, Mr Olmos,' the woman tried to butt in, but he raised a warning finger and she fell silent.

'I was not at home. The card said to come to the post office to collect my item, so I came here, to the post office, to collect my item. But now this Rose tells me that I cannot in fact pick up my item, because it is not here. And why is it not here? Because you've stolen it from me!'

The manager deflated, balloon-like. 'As I told you last time this happened, Mr Olmos, and as I have told you the five or six times before that . . . this isn't the collection office. To pick up your item you have to go to a completely different place. The address was on the card you got. Please . . . please just look at the card properly.'

'I see, so it's all my fault, is it?'

'Well . . . *yes*.'

'You expect me to believe that all this is because I couldn't be bothered to read a card properly? And not because you're a thief? You're not fooling me, Mrs Manager-lady!' His voice soared. 'You're jealous of my antique butter churn, so you stole it from me! You and this Rose person here!'

'We stole *what* from you?'

'The antique butter churn I ordered.'

'I don't even know what that is.'

Mr Olmos held his hand at waist height. 'About this big. You use it to make butter.'

'And why did you order that?'

'Because making butter is my new hobby!'

'Mr Olmos,' the woman pleaded, 'if you'd just go to the collection office, I'm sure that they can help you find your . . . butter churn.'

'I see. You'll send me away so that you can get my churn to a safe house where it'll never be seen again.'

'That's insane. Rose and I don't want a butter churn.'

'And you call yourself a manager! The only thing you *manage* is being a massive pain in my backside!'

Alex burst out laughing. He couldn't help himself. It was like water breaking through a dam.

The old man's head snapped round towards the source of the laughter. He fixed Alex with a stare. His eyes were so dark as to be almost opal-black. Something – the ceiling lights or perhaps a car passing outside – reflected in them, and for a moment it was almost if as they burnt with a deep fire.

And then the man winked. It was a fraction of a second – so brief it was almost nothing. But it had definitely been a wink. Something familiar and conspiratorial, as if he was letting Alex in on the joke. As if the whole thing was just for fun. As if complaining like this was the man's hobby.

'Mr Olmos,' said the manager. 'Why don't I call the collections office and see if your parcel is there? I'm sure we can get this sorted out.'

Mr Olmos turned back to her and thought for a second. Fingers drummed on the counter. 'That would be acceptable,' he said at last, and stepped to one side.

'Next please,' said Rose.

And Alex went to buy a suit.

7

'Have a good day,' said his dad, reaching over to give Alex's shoulder a squeeze.

Alex forced a grin. He was dreading school, as he had every day since the Incident, but he could at least try and return the effort.

'Thanks for dropping me off,' he said.

'No worries.' His dad paused and gave a shrug. 'I've missed this, mate. We should do it more often.'

'That would be good.'

'Nice, being able to have a good chat.'

The journey had only been five minutes, but actually it *had* been nice. His dad hadn't been eying his phone or droning on about the people he worked with.

'And I'm sorry about Saturday,' his dad said. 'I know

you were disappointed.'

'Honestly, it's fine.'

'Can I tell you something, Alex?'

He nodded.

'You looked bloody great in that suit.'

This time Alex's smile was completely for real. His dad *got it*. How important the competition was. He was just busy a lot of the time.

His classmates flowed around the car, forming into twos and threes. Into packs. Nina Simone sang on the radio.

'What's up first today, then?'

'PE,' Alex said, willing the conversation to stretch just a little longer.

'Football?'

'I think so, yeah.'

'Still not a fan?' His dad chuckled.

'It's not really my thing.'

'Freddie still plays though?'

Alex tried not to flinch. 'Yeah, of course.'

'Good little player, Freddie is.'

Alex didn't answer. His dad liked reading about football in the paper. He never read about magic at all, and the book about Houdini that Alex had got him for Christmas still sat, unopened and spine intact, on the coffee table.

'Been ages since I saw Fred. You can have people to the house whenever you want. You know that, right?'

'Sure, of course. Thanks, Dad.'

'Well, work hard.'

'I will.'

'And how about we make a deal? I'll try and drop you at least one day a week from now, OK?'

Alex's stomach tightened. He wanted to believe it.

'You're a good boy. Show them what you're made of, yeah?'

'Thanks, Dad. I'll see you tonight.'

'Did you hear?'

'Hear what?' panted Alex.

He was jogging next to a boy named Johnny Fish, also known as Fishy, Fishface, Trout and, increasingly – to some of the girls – Fish the Dish. They both glanced up as Mr King gave a sharp blast of his whistle, but it was aimed at another of their classmates, who had taken a short cut across the penalty box instead of running around the end of the pitch.

'Freddie's leaving,' said Fishface.

'What do you mean, leaving?'

'Like, moving away,' he replied.

'You're joking? Where to?'

'There's some aunt or something. Being sent to live with her. Mrs Taylor went mental when she got that call last week.'

'Fred's being sent away because of me?' said Alex, horrified.

'Not just you, though, is it? Pushed Dev Varma into a locker the other day. Three days internal exclusion for that.'

There was another shriek from Mr King's whistle. 'Warner! Fish! Are we running or are we having a chat?' The two boys went quiet and sped up.

No more Freddie. It was almost unbelievable. Freddie had always been there. Always. The two children had latched on to each other in nursery; driving their parents mad by bursting into tears when they were separated at the end of the day. Their friendship had grown with them. It was Freddie who'd put an arm around Alex when his mother moved out. Freddie who'd been there while his dad pulled further and further away.

But, ever since the Incident, there had been a different Freddie. It was Freddie who'd chased him through the streets. Freddie, whose kick had left a palm-sized bruise on his leg. Freddie, who'd got other the other kids whispering that Alex was, well, a bit weird, right, what with all the magic and stuff . . .

He fell into line with the other boys. Their boots made a moonscape of the grass.

'Right then, you two,' said Mr King. 'If you've finished your mothers' meeting? You can go and put these cones out for me.'

Alex sighed and broke into a run, only to find himself immediately tripping over an outstretched leg, which sent him sprawling on the ground. James Gilfoy smirked down at him. The rest of the class erupted in laughter. They looked dangerous, he thought, with mud-stained kit and savage eyes.

Mr King gave another blast of the whistle and everyone fell silent.

'I saw that, Gilfoy,' he called. 'Come and see me after class. Now come on, Warner, get to it!'

Alex dragged himself to his feet.

8

The end of the week. Finally. Just one sleep till the heats.

Alex watched from a front window as the other pupils drained into the streets or on to the buses parked outside. The school was empty, apart from the janitors cleaning up the day's mess and teachers still working away in their classrooms.

He made his way through vacant corridors that smelt of damp cloth and detergent. The click of shoes on floor echoed down the passageways. His skin prickled. He felt as if eyes were peering at him through the metal slits of the lockers that lined the walls. A set of double doors banged behind him, sending his heart hammering up into his throat. *Just the wind*, he told himself. Just a breeze sent swirling by a door opening somewhere. He had a sudden horror of being trapped; of everyone going home and the school being locked with him inside; snared in a maze of hallways and stalked by some awful creature.

Alex pulled a coin from his pocket. The metal was cool on his skin. As he walked, he made it vanish and reappear, vanish and reappear. The repetition calmed him – but what use was a coin trick when confronted by a monster?

At last he reached the drama studio and pushed his way inside, bolting the door behind him. It was a large, square room with a high roof and a balcony running around three sides. The brick walls were painted black, and metal bars – strung with theatre lamps – hung from the ceiling. A small rake of seating faced towards a low stage.

Alex plugged in the lighting desk and the lamps burst into life, so bright they dazzled him for a moment. He moved the plastic dials down to a more comfortable level, but tiny glowing spots still swam in front of his eyes. At once he was gripped by the memory of those strange creatures in the garden. All week he'd been telling himself that they'd been a figment of his imagination. Or that his tired, scared brain had turned a perfectly normal phenomenon into something strange and other. But he didn't really believe that, did he? He'd seen what he'd seen. Unless he was going completely crazy, and he was sure that wasn't the case. Well, fairly sure, anyway.

He needed to go back. That much was obvious. Tonight, he told himself. He would go back there tonight.

But first he had work to do. He played with the lighting levels until he was happy with the effect, and then jumped up on to the stage. He closed his eyes and took a few deep breaths, trying to push away the panicked thoughts crowding their way in. *There are no monsters in the school.* He shrugged his shoulders hard up to his ears and let them drop. *Loose*, he thought. *You have to be loose.* He rolled his neck, first one way and then the other. He was ready.

It was immediately clear that this dress rehearsal had been a good idea. His fingers grew damp under the hot lights, making everything more difficult. The new pack of cards he'd opened were too slippery to hold properly. He'd lost his usual practice deck somewhere along the line; another thing gone wrong.

'Ladies and gentlemen,' he began, but his voice vanished into the space like a wisp of smoke. 'Ladies and gentlemen!' he tried again. In his head, when he performed, he was smooth, he was suave, he was witty. He could make his audience laugh and he could make them gasp. He was like Houdini with his water cell routine, or Jack Kellar with his famous Shadow World. But, as Alex went through his tricks, the gap between fantasy and reality became starkly clear.

'Focus,' he said out loud. He was comparing himself to the greats, he realized. How could he hope to be great when his thirteenth birthday was still six months away? *I've only got to be good enough to win the heats*, he told himself. But still, the thought of all those people watching – of Jack Kellar watching – made his stomach lurch.

He put one hand on the back wall to steady himself.

'Ladies and gentlemen!' he declared once more, and strode forward with his arms out and palms turned upwards. 'Ladies and gentlemen, I know what you're thinking.' He gathered his voice from down in his guts and projected. It filled the space with a pleasing ring. 'Ladies and gentlemen, I know what you're thinking . . . but that's because I'm psychic. Some people assume it must be difficult, having to listen to other people's thoughts. But actually, it's never bothered me. I'm perfectly content! In fact, I've always been a happy medium . . .'

Alex flowed through the routine, aware only of the lights and the movement of his body. For the final trick one of the audience would pick-a-card-any-card. The pack would be shuffled and reshuffled until, finally, Alex would choose one – getting it wrong, of course. He'd try again . . . wrong once more. By this point the audience would be shifting in their seats, embarrassed. Alex would start to become irate. He'd choose cards, faster and faster, but each one would be wrong. In the end, in a fit of pique, he would snatch the pack from the hand of the audience member . . .

'Oh, for goodness sake, is *this* your card?' he shouted at the empty studio, and threw the deck high, high up into the air. And, when they fluttered down, each and every one of them had transformed into the three of hearts.

He was ready.

9

Alex retraced the route he'd taken the previous week. A yellow sky stretched above him, stained with smears of dark cloud.

This was a bad idea. A very, very bad idea. This was the worst idea, Alex decided, that he'd ever had. He'd almost been rumbled last time and now he was going back for another look. If he was caught he'd be charged with, what? Breaking and entering? How many years in jail could you get for that? *It wasn't fair*, he thought, *the gate had been unlocked*. All right, he'd entered, but the only thing he'd broken was a plant pot.

Previously he'd been running for his life. Now, having more time, he was able to scan the little road of terraced houses. It was familiar, he realized. His dad had brought him here a few years before. There had been a woman who helped write brochures for his company. Her daughter, Alex remembered, had some kind of illness which stopped her going outside. She'd showed him a book of stories she was writing. One of them had been about a circus magician who discovered he had real magic powers. They'd moved away in the end, hadn't they? His dad had been annoyed about having to find someone else to do the job.

The house he was looking for sat at the very end of the road – a corner plot with an L-shaped garden running around the back and side of the building. The black door showed a knocker in the shape of a lion's head and a brass number thirty-three above that.

Alex paused, lead weights in his stomach. Was he really going to do this? Who knew what kind of a person lived there? For all he knew they could be a complete and utter lunatic! But he'd seen things he couldn't explain. Things that made the ordinary world feel as if it was built on quicksand. And that was the point, wasn't it? He had to know.

A small, dark shape slunk past him, slipping away into the gathering night in pursuit of prey. Alex followed in its footsteps, around the corner to the side gate. Satisfied there was no one watching, he turned the metal ring.

It opened.

Just don't get caught, he thought, as he stepped through.

No lights on in the back windows of the house – that was good.

But nothing much in the garden, either. There was the tree. Plants and bushes. A shed stood off to one side, its sloping roof lit by the orange glow of a street light. The small lawn was studded with fallen apples. He pushed at one with his toe and it broke open easily, all slush and rot inside. But nothing else. Nothing out of the ordinary, at least.

Alex could hear the hiss of his own breathing. The thud of his heart.

What if the creatures were hiding? Or maybe they'd just been passing through and had gone somewhere else entirely. Or perhaps – and this seemed like an increasing possibility – he was losing his mind and had imagined the whole thing.

What was he doing? He had to get up early tomorrow for his heat. *Young Magician of the Year!* Jack Kellar! He should be at home doing some last-minute practice, ironing his shirt for the tenth time and getting a good night's sleep. Not sneaking around a stranger's back garden in the hope of encountering some floating balls of fire!

Alex strode back towards the gate but had gone no more than two steps when he felt something. A tickle in his mind. A gentle scratching at a door somewhere right in the centre of his brain as if something wanted to come in. And it was warm. The same warmth he'd felt the last time he was here.

'Hello?' he whispered, and immediately felt foolish. There was no point in speaking, he realized. The thing was hiding. But nearby, he knew.

Hello, he said, with some part of himself deep down inside. *Hello?*

The scratching paused a moment and then came back, more insistently. Alex closed his eyes and reached towards it, searching until his mind met the visitor. The two of them flowed around each other.

Who are you? he asked, and to his shock an answer came back at once. But it wasn't language – or at least any kind of language he could easily understand. It was pictures. Pictures, like old drawings, that flickered through his mind so quickly he could hardly grasp them before they faded away.

A sun-scorched desert.

A torrent of flame.

Birds of prey circling in a perfect blue sky.

A tall figure reaching down with hand outstretched.

What are you trying to tell me? he asked, and the visitor returned something like a giggle.

Alex felt strangely calm. This thing meant no harm. It was as interested in him as he was in it. He tried to forget words and sent pictures of his own back. His house, his school, a pack of cards being shuffled. The mind merging with his own was delighted, pouring over the things he conjured, turning them over to examine

44

them more quickly. *Becoming part of them* in some strange way. He felt the same dizziness as he had the other night but didn't try and pull away from it this time. He went further and deeper into the fire. Further and deeper. Further and deeper . . .

Until all at once he was dragged back to reality by a hand gripping his arm and a voice growling . . .

'Now I've got you, you little vandal.'

10

'Recognize these?'

The man had one hand clamped firmly on Alex's shoulder. The other held a pack of cards. *My practice cards*, he thought with a sinking heart. They must have fallen out of his pocket when he'd tripped into the pot plant.

'Found them. Wondered if you'd be stupid enough to come back for them.'

All at once Alex realized that he knew him. He'd been right before, it seemed. The man *was* a lunatic. But not just any lunatic. A lunatic with coal-black eyes and frizzy grey hair. The very same lunatic he'd seen making a fuss in the post office the weekend before. Mr Elmo, or something like that.

Alex shifted from one foot to the other, wondering how on earth he was going to get out of this.

'What have you got to say for yourself?' snapped the man.

Alex cleared his throat, opened his mouth to speak, but then closed it again and looked down at the ground. A line of ants trooped in and out of a crack in the concrete path.

The old man rolled his eyes. 'You've been sneaking in and out of my back garden. The least you can do is say something.'

'I haven't been sneaking. I've just . . . I mean . . .'

'Well?' he snapped. 'Spit it out.' The man glowered from under bushy eyebrows.

Alex took a deep breath. 'I saw something. Here. In your garden. Can you tell me what it is?'

The man's eyes widened very slightly and his frown grew deeper. 'You broke my plant pot,' he said at last.

'Yes,' Alex agreed. 'I'm sorry about that.'

'Well, then. I suppose you'd better come in.'

Alex hesitated by the back door. He didn't know anything about this person. On the other hand, the old guy was wrinkled as a walnut. He could probably make a break for it should things go wrong.

'You're letting the heat out,' said the man, 'and what's worse, you're letting the cold in.'

Alex stepped inside. A single low-energy bulb

dangled from the ceiling, but it was wrapped in such an ornate shade that barely any light escaped. Still, he could discern enough to make his eyes go wide with amazement. The hallway was crowded beyond belief. It didn't seem dirty in the slightest – in fact, everything was arranged with extraordinary care and neatness – but it was crammed with all sorts of objects. There were stacks of ancient-looking books and, next to them, several crates of old children's comics. By the stairs lay what appeared to be a half-assembled motorbike engine. There was a beekeeper's suit draped over an ice-cream machine and, pinned to the wall, blueprints for some kind of rocket.

But it didn't end there. There was a lathe covered in wood shavings. There was a calligraphy set, a sewing machine and a fossil collection. There were juggling balls, a unicycle and a half-finished five-thousand-piece jigsaw. Ice skates, fishing rods and a saxophone. Just by the front door was a display case in which different types of scorpion were pinned. Alex followed the man through into the lounge which, if anything, was even more crowded. A musty scent hung in the air; strong but not unpleasant.

'I like your train set,' he said at last.

'So, you're the one who knocked over my gladiolus,' said the man.

'What's a gladiolus?'

'Well, it's in the bin now, but it used to be a plant.'

Alex ran his hand over a half-painted plastic model Death Star.

'Don't touch that,' his host snapped. He held up the cards. 'Do you want these back?'

Alex wasn't silly enough to reach for them then and there; he knew he'd have to offer some kind of explanation.

But before he could say anything the man went on, 'I thought about calling the police. I should call the police. I might *still* call the police.'

'Why haven't you?'

The man didn't answer, but his face creased even more than normal, and it occurred to Alex that this was someone who didn't like attention. Someone who wanted to lie low if they possibly could.

'Well? I'm waiting . . .'

Alex explained how he'd run away from Freddie and ducked into the garden to hide. How he'd been startled by a noise and knocked over the pot. As he spoke, the man's face relaxed a touch and Alex could tell he was being believed. One of the useful skills you learnt as a magician was how to read people quickly. But there was something else there too. The old guy seemed relieved, as if he'd been fearing something worse than a kid hiding from a bully.

'But you came back.'

'Yes.'

'Because you saw something.'

Alex nodded. This was the moment. But the man just shrugged and tapped the cards. 'And what are these for? Your hobby?'

'It's a bit more than a *hobby*.'

'Don't say it like that,' said the man. 'Like hobbies aren't important. They are. They're very important. The most important things in some ways. I have lots,' he said proudly, sweeping an arm around the room.

'You've got some amazing stuff. Like, really amazing.'

'So what are the cards for? Gambling?'

'No, I do magic!'

'Ah, you're a sorcerer,' the man said, nodding his understanding.

'I'm not a *sorcerer*. I'm just a magician.'

'And what's the difference?'

'Well, I suppose it's that sorcerers aren't real. I just make coins vanish, that kind of thing.'

The man frowned. 'Show me,' he said, retrieving something from a shelf and flicking it over to Alex. It was a coin, but not like one he'd ever seen before. Maybe collecting old money was another of this crazy person's crazy-person hobbies. Alex tested the weight in his hand and then deftly palmed it, making it seem as if had melted into thin air.

From nowhere, a crinkle-cut smile broke across the man's face and he clapped his hands together like a young child. 'Bravo,' he shouted. 'Good! Very good indeed! You can do others?'

Alex nodded.

'And you're sure it's just a trick? Not real magic?'

'Of course. I mean, there's no such thing as real magic. Like, when Jack Kellar does his Shadow World, he's not *actually* opening a portal to another dimension.'

'Well, what's he doing then?'

'No one knows. That's why it's such a good trick.'

The man scratched at his wiry beard. 'Mr Olmos,' he said at last. 'You can call me Mr Olmos. On account of that being my name.'

11

'One more time,' said Mr Olmos.

'All right then.' Alex fanned out the deck. 'Pick a card.'

'This time,' the old man insisted. 'This time you won't get it.'

'Maybe not.'

'No maybe, Alex Warner – I'm telling you, you won't get it.'

'I got it right the last nine times.'

'You're cheeky. That's interesting. You break into my garden, kill my plant, and then you still have the nerve to be cheeky. Maybe I will call the police after all.'

Alex glanced at the man's face; his eyes were dancing with a mocking kind of light. 'Any card, sir. Any card you want.'

They were sitting together at the kitchen table. Fine cracks snaked their way across the plaster walls. Mr Olmos made a great show of his selection; calloused fingers walking back and forth along the edge of the deck. Eventually he plucked one.

'Four of clubs,' said Alex instantly.

'You saw!'

'I did not.'

'You cheated!'

'A magician never cheats.'

'A magician,' said Mr Olmos, 'does nothing but cheat. Nothing but tricks, isn't that right?'

'Well, yes, but—'

'No buts! I am correct. I am always correct, and you are a small child who knows almost nothing about anything, and less than that about most other things.'

Alex couldn't help but smile.

Mr Olmos rose from the table, muttering under his breath as he went, and pulled an old biscuit tin from the cupboard. 'Do you want some tea?' he called.

'What kind of tea is it?' asked Alex.

Mr Olmos showed him the contents of the jar. Inside was a strange mixture of dried plant matter that looked and smelt like the devil's pot-pourri. Alex recoiled in disgust and did his best not to gag.

'I'll take that as a no, then,' said Mr Olmos.

He transferred two heaped teaspoons into a mug,

which he then filled with boiling water. Wisps of steam curled up from the lip of the cup, like foul-smelling spirits.

'What *is* that stuff?' Alex asked, covering his mouth with the end of one sleeve.

'Special tea,' replied Mr Olmos.

'And you like it?'

The old man rolled his eyes. 'Of course I don't *like* it,' he said. 'What kind of idiot boy are you? It's awful. It's vile. You think it smells bad? You should taste it. It's like something that came out of a toilet.'

'So why have it?'

'It's good for me.'

'So's fruit,' Alex shot back. 'Maybe try that instead.'

Mr Olmos paused, and it may have been that the slightest hint of a smile tugged at the corners of his lips.

'I don't like you very much, Alex Warner,' he said. 'But I dislike you less than some other people. And less than I did ten minutes ago.'

'Thank you. I think.'

Mr Olmos raised the cup as if to say cheers and knocked the whole fetid brew down in one go. 'Horrendous,' he said with satisfaction. 'Truly and deeply horrendous.'

There was only so long they could go on avoiding the subject. It was all very well to be chatting about magic tricks and weird teas, but there was really only one thing that Alex wanted to know about. It was Mr Olmos who brought it up at last.

'You were in my garden last week.'

He picked at the skin on the back of his hand and didn't quite look at Alex as he spoke. The atmosphere in the room had changed in some small but definite way. Thicker, somehow. Heavier.

'Last week,' Mr Olmos repeated to himself.

Alex hardly dared to breathe.

'I let them out,' the old man went on. 'I do that, you see. I let them out every evening. It's risky, I know that, but then I can't keep them locked away the whole time, can I? And besides, they know to stay low down where no one can see them from the road.'

He gave a sudden laugh and slapped his palm on the table.

'I suppose I should have locked the side gate!' he said. And then, quieter, 'So you saw them. And you're wondering what they are . . .'

Mr Olmos fell silent. Utterly still. His face was worn leather.

Alex stayed quiet, sure that pushing too hard would mean disaster.

At last the old man blew a long breath from between pursed lips and looked up. Alex was again struck by the depth of those nearly black eyes. There seemed to be worlds behind them.

'I've been thinking about it,' said Mr Olmos. 'About

what to tell you. I could say nothing, and hope you forget about it. I could give you some crazy story you wouldn't believe, and then you'd most likely go off and tell all your friends, and they'd come sniffing around and then where would I be?'

All my friends, Alex thought, and a bitter little taste rose in the back of his throat.

The man cleared his throat and went on, 'So, I'm not going to do that. There's a bit of me that thinks I must be a mad person. But then there's another bit of me that *knows* I'm a mad person, and that maybe being mad isn't such a bad thing from time to time. Do you see what I'm saying?'

Alex chewed at his bottom lip. 'No,' he said at last. 'I don't know what you're saying at all.'

'I'm saying that you saw something you weren't meant to see. And if I pretend to you it's not a big deal you're just going to think it's a big deal anyway. So, what I'm going to do is show you just how big a deal it is and hope your socks are knocked so far off you agree it's best to keep it quiet. You get it?'

This time Alex nodded.

'Well then,' said Mr Olmos. 'Hold on to your hat. And, I suppose, to your socks.'

The shed was bolted with the biggest padlock Alex had ever seen. It was the size of a man's fist – if the man in question was a bare-knuckle boxer with a genetic condition that caused his hands to grow to an extraordinary size.

It was just as strange inside. In Alex's experience, sheds were usually full of cobwebs and bags of fertilizer. Mr Olmos's shed was pristine, however. In fact, in comparison to the barely contained chaos of the house, it was quite shockingly tidy. There were thick red curtains blocking the two small windows. On the back wall hung a painting of mountains rising out of red-sand desert. Alex remembered seeing an old easel propped up at the foot of the stairs back inside. There was a patterned rug on the floor and the room was heady with the scent of woodsmoke and incense.

In front of the picture was a heavy table, on which sat a chest. It was made of wood so dark it was almost black; inlaid with an intricate pattern of silver-white discs that seemed to glow.

'Mother of pearl,' said Mr Olmos. 'Quite the looker, isn't she?'

Alex glanced at him. Back in the house the man had been a ball of nervous energy, swinging from outrage to laughter and back again. He'd swung his arms around as he talked, and his face had rolled constantly from expression to expression. Now though, all that was gone. It was like a layer of varnish had been stripped away to reveal the timber underneath. His eyes shone like jet beads and he seemed calm; almost serene.

Alex stayed by the door, still half-fearful that he had been lured into some terrible trap.

Mr Olmos produced a small golden key and slid it into the lock. There was a gentle click which Alex felt as much as heard. His whole body was tingling, as if the air was charged with static. The man turned, and beckoned. Alex told his legs to move. Forced himself forward. He was desperate to look, to understand what he'd seen, and yet somehow, he knew that if he did then nothing would be the same again.

'You have to understand,' said Mr Olmos, 'that no one else in the world knows what's in this box.' He rested one hand on it. His skin was like an old map – criss-crossed with fine lines; veins rising like mountain ranges. 'No one at all.'

'Then why me?' asked Alex.

Mr Olmos was silent for a few moments. Cars grumbled past on the road outside. The air in the shed was warm and still.

'I don't know,' he said at last and shook his head, almost sadly. 'But we'll see what they make of you, won't we? They'll tell me if I've made a mistake.' He turned the key in the lock. 'Ready?'

Before Alex could reply, Mr Olmos opened the box.

Alex looked down into the chest. The wood inside was buffed and polished to a mirror finish. There were three things in there. The same three he'd seen the week before, he assumed, although now they looked quite different. In the garden, they'd seemed like vivid balls of fire, but now they were more like embers, gently glowing black and red.

One of the creatures stirred, drifting across the bottom of the box. It changed shape as it went, like a raindrop running down a window frame. Alex felt that scratching inside his head again and couldn't help but smile. This was the one he'd bonded with before Mr Olmos had grabbed him.

'What are they?' he breathed.

To his amazement the old man burst out laughing. It wasn't a wry chuckle either, rather a full and round belly laugh. For one horrible moment Alex feared the whole thing was some kind of bizarre practical joke. It was all he could do to stop himself from turning to look for a hidden camera.

'What is it?' he asked. 'Why are you doing that?'

Mr Olmos sucked in a lungful of air and steadied himself. 'I'm sorry,' he said. 'I don't know where that came from. It's just . . . how can I explain it? I have no idea how to even begin!'

'Are they some kind of firefly?' Alex asked.

Mr Olmos went blank for a second, and then exploded. '*Firefly?* Some kind of *firefly?*' His face flushed dark. 'Fireflies are just bugs whose bums light up. These are not *fireflies!*'

'I was just asking.'

'These are *ifrit!*'

'If–what?'

'*Ifrit!* They are fire spirits!'

'Fire spirits?'

'Fire spirits! Spirits of fire!'

'And you keep them in your garden?'

Mr Olmos faltered a little. 'Well, obviously!' he barked at last.

'But there's no such thing as fire spirits.'

'You could have fooled me!' Mr Olmos said, pointing to the box. He took a breath and went on, more quietly. '*Jinn.* Have you heard of them, Alex? They're magical creatures, and the *ifrit* are amongst the most powerful of their kind. They've existed since the dawn of time. They live to be thousands of years old. And, yes, three of them are currently living in my shed.'

'When you say *jinn*, do you mean . . . genies?'

'According to you and to Disney, yes. But where I come from they are called *jinn*.'

'Like, you trap them in a lamp and they grant you wishes?'

'I'd like to see you try and put a full-grown *ifrit* in a bottle; it would barbecue your head in about two seconds flat. But these are only young. Infants, really.'

'They're magic,' Alex said in wonder. 'They're real magic.'

'Boy, if only you knew the veiled mysteries and ancient power you're in the presence of now. And you call them *fireflies . . .*'

At that moment one of the *jinn* leapt into the air, kindling into a ball of flame as it went. Alex just about kept from screaming, but he stumbled back against the wall of the shed. Rough wood against his hands. Searing heat against his face. The *ifrit* was right in front of him, so bright that lights exploded and swam before his eyes.

'Don't be afraid,' said Mr Olmos. 'Put your hand out.'

'Will it burn me?'

'Not unless it wants to.'

'And what if it wants to?'

'Then you'll get burnt, won't you?'

Alex slowly extended his arm and the *ifrit* alighted on his upturned palm. He waited for pain but felt nothing apart from a wonderful warmth coursing through his body.

Hello again, he thought.

And then, as if a switch had been flicked, he felt himself once again falling through a flame-wreathed darkness. When Alex opened his eyes he had no idea if he'd been standing there for seconds or days. Mr Olmos's eyes were wide, his mouth open. Alex looked down at the *jinn*. It was as if there was a thread strung between them now, invisible but real. The connection they'd almost made before was complete now. Real. He tried once more to send an image to the creature – one of him standing on stage. It was easier now. He felt the thought flow out of him and into the *ifrit*. And as that happened the creature changed shape. Alex and the old man gasped in unison, because there in front of them, hanging in the air and drawn in fire, was the image of a boy in a suit, holding a deck of cards in his hand.

Neither of them took their eyes off the spirit. Alex waited a moment and then changed the picture in his head to that of a jaguar. The flames twisted and morphed into the form of a prowling panther. It threw its head back and uttered a silent roar.

'It's copying me,' said Alex. 'It's copying my thoughts!'

Although, he realized, that wasn't quite true. The thing in his hand wasn't a mirror, only reflecting what was in front of it. It was adding its own details to the sketches in Alex's head. He began to cycle through images in his mind's eye: a bear, a motorcycle, a grand stately home. He would conjure the picture and then somehow reach out and give it to the *ifrit*, as if he were placing wooden blocks in the correctly shaped holes.

An otter, a book, a fairy-tale castle. Each time the spirit would change into whatever it was he'd thought of. A car, a house, his father's face. Alex cried out. He hadn't meant to think that last one. It had just jumped into his head and now there it was in front of him, wreathed in flame. He shuddered and felt something disconnect deep down in the middle of him. Bond broken, for now. The jinn settled back within the chest.

Alex realized he'd barely been breathing. 'Do they always do that?' he whispered.

Mr Olmos gave a little shake of the head. 'I assume I'll be seeing you again then, Mr Warner?'

12

The train charged through the few miles of green belt separating Hatford Cross from sprawling outer London. The seasons were all mixed up today – early autumn leaves glowing yellow in the light of a warm sun. Here and there trees that had got ahead of their fellows flamed vivid orange-red.

Alex checked his watch for perhaps the tenth time in ten minutes. It was all right; he wouldn't be late. Unless the train crashed, of course. That was unlikely maybe, but it could easily break down. The train could break down and if it did there was no way he'd make the competition in time. No way he'd be able to get through to the national finals and no chance of meeting Jack Kellar. Panic mingled with anger. He shouldn't even *be* on this stupid train.

Alex had dreamt the night before that Hatford Cross was ablaze: that the town hall smouldered in ruins, that the gargoyles on the abbey walls melted in the heat, and that every house on every street was turned into a flaming torch. He'd woken to find his sheets were soaked with sweat.

Breakfast had been chocolate spread on toast, eaten while pacing up and down the garden path, staring at the moon, which still hung in the purple-blue morning sky. He'd spent an hour running over his routine until, finally, there had come the squeak of floorboards above his head. Alex brewed a pot of coffee, buttered some more toast and left both things on the table in front of his dad's favourite chair.

'Morning, Al,' he'd said, as he came in a few minutes later, wearing boxer shorts and a T-shirt.

'Morning, Dad.'

'Sorry about last night. We'll do movie night next week for sure.'

Alex shook his head. *No problem.* 'How was work?'

His dad snorted. 'Never ends.'

And you like it that way. The thought had popped into Alex's head before he could stop it, and he immediately felt a flush of shame. *That's not true*, he told himself. His dad had to work long hours. Now that his mum was gone, he was the only one providing for them. It wasn't his fault he had a demanding job.

'They've even got me working today,' his dad said, and Alex's breath hitched to a momentary stop.

'What do you mean?'

'Got to have lunch with a client. Some pub out north of town.'

'But . . . it's . . . it's Saturday.'

'You know how it is, Al, if a big client wants to meet me . . .'

'But it's Saturday!'

'What can I do?'

You can say no! screamed the voice in Alex's head. *You can tell them you need a day off! You can tell them you have to take your son to his competition!* He looked around at the calendar on the wall. There it was, written plain as anything on today's date – *Young Magician of the Year*. Alex felt as if all the air had been let out of him. His dad had promised. He'd promised to take him, promised to watch, promised to support him, promised that, win or lose, they'd go for dinner together in London afterwards. And now he'd forgotten all about it.

'You all right, Al? Looking a bit . . . I don't know.'

His throat was so tight that for a moment Alex hadn't known if he'd be able to force the words out. 'I'm fine, yeah. I get it. Work's work.'

'Work *is* work,' his dad agreed, chomping into his toast.

Alex had changed into his suit, packed his things and left before his father could say anything. He'd walked the two miles to the station and paid for a ticket with the card he had for emergencies. The beautiful day seemed wrong somehow; almost mocking. But at least the sun had dried the tears on his cheeks.

13

'And you are?' asked the woman, not looking up.

'Alex Warner.'

She scanned the list for so long Alex wondered if she was blind. *He* could see his name, plain as day. There were only fifteen people on there and they were all in alphabetical order. At last, though, she found it and, with what sounded very much like a sigh of disgust, ticked it off. He was the last one to arrive, it appeared.

'Parent or guardian?' she asked.

'I'm neither,' he said. She turned her puckered face towards him and raised her eyebrows. 'I mean, it's just me,' Alex conceded, smile fading.

'No parent or guardian. I see.' A bell rang, high and

shrill. 'Go through there and take a seat in one of the front two rows.'

Alex nodded.

'Quickly, then!' she scolded.

The theatre foyer smelt of wet dog. Walls blushed off their paint in shame. A girl sat behind the box office counter, completely engrossed in her phone while on the other side was a stand selling T-shirts for 'The Bell Jar – A New Musical!' Alex followed the threadbare carpet up a flight of stairs to a door with a laminated A4 'Young Magician of the Year' sign stuck to it.

As he stepped inside he felt the blanket of gloom slip from his shoulders. *This* was what he'd come for. The auditorium wasn't huge, but it was shabbily grand. The front lip of the dress circle and the boxes high on each wall were patterned and gilded. High above, beyond the lighting bars, was a ceiling rose that Alex thought must be the equal of anything in the world. There were perhaps thirty or forty adults scattered amongst the red seats raking down towards the stage. He could see his fellow competitors lined up in the first two rows.

'Come on, come on,' called a voice from the stage. It came from a man in a velvet jacket and enormous bow tie. 'Well, don't just stand there!' He consulted the clipboard in his hand. 'You must be Warner.'

Alex saw heads turn towards him.

'Well, are you or aren't you?'

'Yes,' he said, hurrying down to the second row and

ignoring the smirks of the other contestants. They were mostly boys, he saw, and mostly in suits just like his. One kid had draped himself in a purple cloak and top hat however, whilst another was wearing what looked suspiciously like a Hogwarts school uniform (Gryffindor). On balance Alex felt satisfied with his choice of simple black jacket and tie. He slid into the seat next to Hogwarts and nodded hello.

'Don't worry,' said the other boy, exposing a mouth still missing half its adult teeth, 'I'm not a real wizard.' He giggled, as if this were the naughtiest, funniest thing in the world. Alex smiled politely.

'My name . . .' said the walking bow tie up on stage, 'is James Donaldson.' He paused, as if for applause that never came. 'General Secretary of the Magic Society,' he went on. 'Welcome to this, the London and South-East heat of *Young Magician of the Year*. I am your chairman of judges and this year will be ably assisted by a man who needs no introduction, I'm sure.' A ripple ran through the audience. 'Contestants, the rules are as follows. Each contestant shall have five minutes to perform their routine. This cannot be extended by any contestant for any reason. There will be a short interval after the first eight contestants, after which the remaining seven contestants shall perform. Once all contestants have performed, the judges shall deliberate, after which we will inform you which contestant has been judged the winner and the aforementioned winning contestant will progress to the national final, in this very theatre, in two weeks' time. Contestants, I hope that's all clear?'

The audience stared in slack-jawed wonder. How could one man be so unutterably dull? And say the word 'contestant' so many times?

'Good,' said James Donaldson, undeterred. 'And now for something a little bit special . . .' He trotted down the stairs at the side of the stage and took a seat. The lights went down and there was rustling as the audience shifted in their seats. The theatre was completely dark, but Alex fancied he saw a shape move quickly across the stage. He leant forward. It couldn't be, could it? He was a judge, yes, but they'd said nothing about him performing.

A spotlight came on, throwing a narrow cone of light. And there he was. Jack Kellar.

For a while Kellar did nothing but look out at the audience with that familiar half-smile playing at the corners of his mouth. Then he gave a slow nod and the lights were raised a little.

'There is,' he announced in a soft voice that some- how filled the room, 'a world other than this one. There is . . . a shadow world.'

The contestants around Alex erupted in applause and he realized that *he* was clapping too; almost bouncing out of his seat in excitement. The Shadow

World! Kellar's most famous and most baffling trick. In the seat next to him, Hogwarts looked as if his eyes would pop out of his head.

The magician extended one arm and made an odd movement with his hand, as if he were taking hold of some invisible object. As he did so his fingers seemed to puncture the air itself, releasing silver-grey shafts of light that lanced out in all directions. He placed his other hand alongside the first and pulled. The audience gave a collective gasp as a gap appeared, hanging in the centre of the stage about a metre from the floor. Alex could see the magician's lips moving; murmuring something over and over again.

At last Jack Kellar stood back, taking a handkerchief from his top pocket and wiping beads of sweat from his brow. Beside him now was a small, impossible doorway from which more of that strange light spilt out over the stage. Through the opening Alex could see what looked like a grey late-evening sky; all swirling darkness and storm clouds.

He'd seen this before, of course, but only on a screen, and there it was all too easy to write it off as a special effect, no different from something you'd see in a film. But now, watching it live, Alex's mouth went dry and his skin puckered with goosebumps. He couldn't take his eyes off the roiling shadows revealed by the doorway. They were on stage, just a few metres from him, but also seemed be further away than the most distant star.

It's real...

The thought came suddenly and without warning, startling him. Of course it wasn't real! It was a trick like any other. There were reams of speculation about how Kellar achieved his Shadow World. Some said he had tiny projectors concealed in his sleeves, others that he actually hypnotized his audience en masse. The mystery was one of the reasons Alex loved him – no one else could create an illusion as convincing as this.

And yet, seeing it for himself, Alex was swamped by a horrible sense of unease. He felt as if he were having a glimpse of something no person was meant to see; something awesome but terrible. He fancied he could hear noises coming from the gap – an insane howling, like the cry of some unspeakable creature.

And then Jack Kellar climbed through the gap and vanished.

Alex could feel his heart thudding inside his ribcage. Panic washed around inside him. He glanced over at Hogwarts, who was smiling. Smiling! Didn't he see what was happening? Didn't he see that this was all horribly wrong? Hadn't he heard the screams in the darkness?

A new opening appeared at the back of the stage, spilling more of that awful grey light. Slow seconds passed, and then Jack Kellar emerged once more, with tendrils of dark smoke trailing behind him. He turned, raised his arms and – with one deafening clap of his hands – the gap in the air vanished.

Alex looked around, his mouth hanging open. They were cheering. They were . . . they were cheering. But of course they were. Why wouldn't they? It was the Shadow World! Alex himself had watched variations of it a thousand times online. There was nothing sinister about it! It was just a trick, just a show!

And then Alex was on his feet with all the others, hammering his palms together. His fears had been ridiculous. *He* had been ridiculous. It was like thinking there was someone in your room at night only to switch on the lights and realize it was just a chair piled high with dirty clothes. He laughed and shouted and cheered.

Jack Kellar came to the front of the stage, smiling. 'Well, that's about enough of me,' he said. 'Now it's time for the real show.'

14

The security light pinged on as Alex made his way down the driveway that evening. A stiff wind had picked up and the ground was scattered with fallen leaves. His key wouldn't turn, and for a second he imagined his dad had changed the locks. But it was just the metal sticking, of course. He shoved.

There was music coming from the back of the house, and raised voices too. Alex started towards his bedroom but was pulled up short by his dad's voice.

'Is that you? Hello, anyone there? Hellooo?' Laughter, harsh and loud, like metal screws rattling in a tin.

The black radiator gave a gurgling chuckle at his misfortune. Alex glared at it. He decided to ignore the call, but just then his dad appeared in the kitchen doorway.

'Thought I heard you come in,' he said.

'Sorry, I won't disturb.'

'Where have you been? You just vanished this morning. Thought it was one of your tricks.'

A few seconds of silence ticked by as realization made its way into his dad's brain. His mouth fell open. He looked Alex up and down, taking in the suit and tie, and scrunched his hair with one hand. 'Mate,' he began, 'I'm so sorry . . .'

Alex put his rucksack down at the foot of the stairs.

'Mate!' his dad tried again. 'I completely forgot. Just this morning . . . You know how it is with work sometimes. Takes over a bit. You know?'

'It's fine, Dad.'

'But you went? You went to your competition?'

'Yes.'

'To London? You went all the way into London on your own?' *Was that a flicker of concern?* Alex wondered. His dad was still rummaging in his hair, as if he'd find an answer in there somewhere.

'It was fine. Easy. Just got the train.'

'That's good. And you got there on time?'

'I said it was fine.'

'Well, that's good.' He shifted from one foot to the other. 'And how did you get on? I mean, how did it go? Was it OK? How were the other kids?'

'They were nice.' Alex thought about Hogwarts in his ridiculous cloak.

'But you got on OK? Did you? You know . . .' He waved his arms around in a circular motion. 'You know?'

Alex shrugged.

'Oh Al, I'm sorry. But look, you did your best, right? You practised and you did your best. Sometimes that's all you can do. Isn't it?'

They faced each other down the long hallway. The seconds hobbled past far too slowly. Another gale of rough laughter erupted from the back room and Alex saw his dad's eyes flick that way.

'It's all right, Dad,' he said, grateful for the chance to escape. 'You get back to it. I'm tired anyway.'

'Tired? It's only, what, eight o'clock?' His dad raised an eyebrow. 'We've got pizza.'

Alex shook his head.

'What? You're telling me you don't want pizza? You love pizza.' He spread his arms wide. 'Come and get it while it's hot!'

His father flashed a wolfish sort of grin that Alex hadn't seen for a long time and without meaning to he found himself smiling back. Pizza it was.

It was nice, he had to admit. He'd expected his dad's clients to be awful sneering creatures but actually they seemed, well . . . normal. There were four of them altogether, including Alex and his father, but enough pizza for twice as many people. They ate straight from the boxes, all spread out on the dining table.

'Your dad tells me you're into magic,' said one of the adults – Tony – in between mouthfuls of pepperoni. Bits of tomato and mozzarella clung to his beard.

Alex glanced up in surprise.

'I do talk about you, you know,' his dad said.

'Hang on, what are we saying here?' asked the other man, who may have been called either Don or Ron or Rob or Bob. 'Like, are you just pulling flowers out of your sleeves or can you make the Tower of London disappear?'

'Somewhere in the middle, I guess.'

'Come on then, let's see something,' said Possibly Don.

'Yeah, let's see something,' agreed Tony.

His dad gave an encouraging nod.

Alex shrugged, rose and retrieved his jacket from the back of his chair.

'Getting dressed up for it!' shouted Possibly Don, clapping his hands together.

'I want you to think of a number,' Alex said to Tony, who was the quieter of the two. 'Any number—'

'One hundred million, five billion and seventy-nine,' cut in Don, slapping his own knee in amusement.

'Any number between one and a hundred.'

'All right, got it,' said Tony.

'Now I want you to focus entirely on that number—'

'Yes, Tone,' interrupted Don once more, 'entirely on the number. Don't be thinking about your golf handicap or whether you've left the kettle on.'

'You made me forget it now!'

Alex felt himself shrink a little. They seemed different all of a sudden; like dogs play-fighting. He didn't want to be in the middle when one of them turned.

'It's OK,' he said. 'It's a silly trick anyway.'

'No, come on,' said Don. 'You promised us magic. Hey, can you pull a rabbit from a hat? What about a lady?'

'Can he pull a lady from a hat?' said Alex's dad, and they all laughed this time.

'Can he saw a lady in half, I was going to say. Every decent magician can saw a lady in half. It was the Great Sparaducci first did that, wasn't it, Alex? The Great Sparaducci?'

'There's no such person,' said Alex quietly.

'What's that?'

'I said, there's no such person.'

His dad rolled his eyes. 'Don't worry, Alex, he's just messing around,' he said.

'Come on, take a joke!' said Don.

Alex felt his blood light on fire, spreading through his chest and over his face. He turned away and started for the door.

'Sorry, mate,' Tony chipped in. 'We'll play along, I promise.'

'Come on, it was just a joke!' his dad called. 'Al. Al!'

Alex felt something pop inside his head. 'It's *Alex*,' he shouted. His words pinged off the walls. 'It's always been *Alex*.'

The room was deathly silent. The three men stared with jaws hanging slackly open, in a way that was almost funny. Almost, but not quite. He turned and ran for the stairs.

The handle turned halfway, then stopped. A moment later there was a knock on the door. Alex waited a few moments. 'Come in,' he said at last. His dad shuffled into the room, hands thrust deep in his pockets and blotches of red about his throat.

'What was all that then?' his father asked.

Alex shook his head and stared at the ceiling, fearing that if he spoke any more he'd cry.

'Al. Alex, I mean. About what happened.' For a moment Alex felt a little spark of hope. But then his dad went on, 'Never embarrass me like that in front of clients again. Do you understand me? I said, *do you understand me?*'

Alex rolled on to his side and stared out into the night. He heard the door swing firmly shut and footsteps retreating. Finally, after a few minutes he slid off the bed and opened his rucksack. Inside was a trophy. On it was some writing:

WINNER
YOUNG MAGICIAN OF THE YEAR
LONDON AND SOUTH-EAST HEAT

15

They travelled in silence. Nothing but the crunch of tyres on tarmac; the rise and fall of the engine.

A woman jogged by on a Sunday morning run, her ponytail swishing behind. Two older ladies walked arm in arm, heads turned towards one another, intent on their conversation. A dog strained at the leash while its owner talked on his phone.

Alex cracked the window just a touch. The thick, musty damp of sodden leaves. He sucked in a breath; felt the coolness of the breeze on his face.

'Shut that, will you, Alex?' said his dad. 'It stops the air conditioning from working.'

Why do you need air conditioning when you can smell the air? Alex wondered, and didn't respond.

'Alex,' his father insisted.

He pressed the button and turned to face front.

'Do you want to put the radio on?' his dad asked at last.

'If you want,' Alex replied.

'I'm asking if *you* want to.'

'It's up to you.'

A sharp exhalation. 'Suit yourself.'

The radio stayed off.

They hadn't spoken about the night before, the two of them. Alex didn't know what to say. The trophy would sit on his desk. It wasn't something to be hidden. And besides, Dad never went into his room anyway. He'd considered telling him. Knew he *should* tell him. But didn't. Wouldn't, he supposed.

They turned on to a wider road. A sudden blast of acceleration pinned him back into his seat for a few seconds. Lampposts whipped by: one, two, three, four, five, six, seven, eight. He let his vision blur until they melted into waving grey lines of nothing, and his eyes ached just a little.

He thought of the *jinn*, safe in their box. Slumbering. Smouldering. Alive.

Duchess, his mother's cat, was sprawled on the garden wall – a gently heaving mass of sinew and black fur. Two sparrows pecked at the grass for food, seemingly unconcerned.

The car rolled to a stop and they sat in silence for a moment.

'Look,' his dad began, at last. 'Look, mate,' he tried again. 'Last night wasn't great, right?'

Alex shook his head.

'I forgot your show. I can't believe I forgot your show. I get why you're annoyed with me. No, not annoyed. I get why you're angry. Furious, probably. I would be in your shoes. And I shouldn't have let those guys mess around like that, but they were honestly just teasing you. But look, I'm sorry.'

Hollowness. A gaping hole somewhere in the middle.

'So,' his dad went on, 'are we good?'

Alex nodded. 'We're good,' he replied.

His dad reached out to ruffle his hair but stopped just short and gave him an awkward pat on the shoulder instead. 'You're not a little boy any more, are you?'

Alex supposed that wasn't the kind of question that wanted or needed an answer, so instead he just gave his best imitation of a smile.

'Say hi to your mum for me.'

'I will.'

'And have fun.'

Duchess opened one septic-yellow eye as Alex passed. For one brief moment he considered stroking her but just then she yawned, giving a long glimpse of her needle-sharp teeth, and he thought better of it. One of the sparrows plucked a worm from the damp ground and fluttered off in victory. The cat gave a look that said, *I let that happen because I'm sleepy. I'll get the cheeky worm-snatcher next time.*

Alex knocked and waited.

It was a cottage really. One storey, of course. Nowhere near as big as their house, but far older, with ivy creeping up the walls and rose bushes in the garden. Alex imagined those plants growing out of control – the branches thickening and twisting, coming to circle the whole place with their wicked thorns, like the castle in the fairy tale.

'Coming, coming!' came the sing-song shout from inside, alongside the squeak of rubber wheels across a floor. Butterflies in his tummy. A slight flush on his face. The sound of keys being jangled and then the door opened.

'Alex!' cried his mother, with that mixture of delight and surprise that he always found odd given he came to visit every other Sunday. He grinned despite himself and bent down to embrace her. The scent of some perfume or other clung to her dress. Alex had no idea what it was, but it smelt powerfully of *her*. He would know it anywhere. There was something else too, a sharper, acrid note. Paint. She was working, then.

'Come in, darling, come inside,' she said, spinning around and beckoning him through. 'It's vile out there.'

The hallway was dark and gloomy, but wide enough for her wheelchair. The previous owner had apparently had it adapted for her husband before he died. Alex followed his mum through to a large room at the back with a set of wide French doors. Canvases hung all around, covering every spare inch of space, and lying stacked against the walls. There was an easel in the centre of the floor; turned to face the grey autumn light.

'Can I look?' he asked.

'Of course, of course, go ahead!'

Alex faced the current work in progress. It was a whirl of muted colours, like the coming of a storm. Somewhere in there was the image of a man in a suit. There was a station sign next to him reading *Hatford Cross*. The man's face was marked out with a few seemingly careless lines, but he looked to carry the world heavily on his shoulders, and he was utterly, utterly alone. Alex knew his mother's pictures as well as he knew her face.

'Well, what do you think?' she said.

He looked at her. She was the same age as Dad but looked younger. Her skin held barely any lines at all. Her sandy hair – the same shade as his – was twirled into a messy pile on the top of her head.

'It's great,' he said honestly.

'Really?'

'Really.'

'I'm so pleased you said that. Such a relief. I've just been working so much you can't see the wood for the trees, you know?'

'It makes me feel a little sad. Looking at it, I mean. He looks lonely.'

She was nodding, eyes locked on to his. 'Are you hungry?' she asked suddenly, taking his hand in her dry, warm fingers, 'I bet you haven't even had breakfast, have you?'

Alex shook his head.

'Well, come on then, I'll fix us some lunch.'

'It's ready,' she said, shooing him into a chair.

For just a moment everything was still and quiet and Alex felt a nice sort of warmth right in the middle of his body. Steam licked up from the bowl in front of him, and the kitchen hummed with the background smell of roasted coffee. The knots in his stomach unclenched just a little.

A clatter from the back door and Duchess stalked in, tail held high like a car aerial, and long fur puffed out. She flopped down on the floor and promptly fell asleep.

'Silly old thing,' said Alex's mum.

Silly wasn't the word he would have used. *Brutal*, was close to the mark. *Evil*, perhaps. *Psycho*, even.

'So, where is it?' asked Mum.

'Where's what?'

'You know what I'm talking about.'

Alex shook his head.

'Your trophy. What? You didn't think I'd forget about yesterday, did you?'

'No, but . . . but how did you know I'd won?'

'Of course you won. You're my son, and you're brilliant. Plus, you didn't reply to my messages so I called up the theatre to find out. Well?'

Alex fished the *Young Magician* heat-winner's cup from his bag and placed it on the table.

'Will you look at that . . .'

'It's just a lump of plastic.'

'I wish I could have been there. And for the final. It's just this bloody thing. Those old theatres don't do much for people in my situation.' She shook the chair and Alex thought he could see wetness spring up in the corner of her eye. He grabbed for her hand.

'It doesn't matter. I'll tell you all about it after.'

'My son. Young Magician of the Year.'

'I've only won the heat.'

'So far.'

'I probably won't win the whole thing. The standard's really good.'

'They won't be able to resist you, Alex.'

'You have to say that.'

She shook her head and smiled. 'How's your dad?'

'He's good. Working a lot.'

A disapproving sort of grunt. 'What a surprise.'

'It's all right.'

'What did he say about this?' Pointing to the trophy.

'He was pleased, obviously.'

'Must have been nice, seeing him in the audience.'

Colour rose to Alex's cheeks. 'Yeah, it was great.'

'And Freddie?'

'Mum . . .'

'Still giving you problems?'

'It's fine. It's normal. That's just what school's like.'

'You should tell someone.'

'I did.'

'What? Who?'

'Mrs Mutola.'

'And? Has it helped?'

'I told you it wouldn't.'

'But now a teacher knows, they can keep an eye out.'

I'm not in school the whole time, he thought, but kept quiet.

'Come on then, eat up before it gets cold,' she said.

'I've got to go a bit earlier today,' he replied.

'What? Why?'

'I need to practise as much as I can.'

'You can do that here though, can't you?'

'School are letting me use the drama studio.'

Alex felt a little bad for lying to his mother. He didn't like cutting the visit short, but there was somewhere he had to be, and it wasn't school. And so, as the afternoon nudged into evening, Alex found himself back in town, walking up the road past Weston Park. Through the little streets he went until he came to number thirty-three.

He rang the doorbell and waited.

16

Strange how quickly the week fell into a rhythm. Strange how the extraordinary and the ordinary separated themselves and lived side by side. Strange how quickly the unbelievable became almost, if not quite, normal.

Days were spent at school, as ever. School, with all its little victories and setbacks. So routine, so familiar and bewildering. Lessons, teachers and the lunch queue. School, with its pattern of constantly shifting alliances that rose and fell like tiny empires. On Tuesday morning Alex helped Fish with the answers in biology, and in return was invited into a lunchtime game of football. Gilfoy and Down circled the makeshift pitch like sharks, but their prey was safe in a group. For now.

He caught the odd glimpse of Freddie, but not much more than that. He wasn't surprised. With Agnes Taylor on the warpath and a possible change of school looming, his ex-best friend would be trying to keep a low profile. And anyway, there were others to do the dirty work.

And then the afternoons. Running full pelt from the gates and zigzagging through little streets to shake off anyone who might be following. Every sense on full alert. Listening for the whir of bike tyres on tarmac.

Mr Olmos would usher him inside. Every day there was something new in the house. On Monday it was a glass case full of exotic beetles. Already dead, of course – each one pinned to the backboard, with the name of its species printed on a little white card underneath. They looked like weapons of war, Alex thought. Like tanks. On Tuesday there was a set of African drums, and on Wednesday a box full of books – each and every one of which was about Napoleon.

But the main event was the trip to the shed, of course. Opening the box. That feeling of terrified excitement as the three *jinn* woke, flaring up like blown coal and drifting out into the darkening garden. Alex found he could tell them apart, though to the naked eye there was no difference. It was something in the way they *felt*. Different personalities, as distinct from each other as one person to the next.

'What are their names?' he'd asked.

'They don't have them,' Mr Olmos had told him.

'Why not?'

'They will. When they're old enough to choose for themselves.'

With every day that passed Alex found it easier to bond with the *ifrit*, and easiest of all with the one who'd come to him that first night. He would reach towards her and she would respond, merging her thoughts with his. It was a strange thing, the mind of a fire spirit – like a book written in a different language. There was meaning there, but it was hard to see.

She. Alex was sure of it. The other two were male, he felt, but there was something different about her. *His favourite.*

'But how?' he asked Mr Olmos one evening.

'How?'

'How any of this? How . . . just how?'

'How did I come to have three fire spirits in my shed?'

'Yes!'

'Well, that's a good question.'

'OK.'

'Which I'm not going to answer.'

Alex slumped. The female spirit floated to his side. He held out his hand and she came to rest on his palm.

'All you need to know is that I found them quite a while ago. And I promised myself that I'd look after them until the time came.' Mr Olmos nodded, as if confirming it to himself.

'What time?'

'I told you, these *ifrit* are just infants. They have a very long childhood. They're feeding, you see. Getting stronger. Building themselves up until they can ascend.'

'What does that mean?'

'Ascension is when a *jinn* matures. Comes into its full power. When that happens, they can do almost anything.'

'You said "feeding". I haven't seen them eat.'

'Well, it's not like having cats! I don't just put out a bowl of kibble every morning, you stupid boy.'

Alex smirked, and Mr Olmos went on.

'They feed on *this*.' He waved his arm around the garden. 'On the energy in the air. On the crackle of life all around. On the hum of power within every single object, from people to the pebbles on a garden path.'

'And they do this by themselves? I mean, they do it naturally?'

'Of course. *Jinn* don't have parents to look after them like you do.'

Alex swallowed a sudden hard lump in his throat.

'There have been *ifrit* for millions of years. Long before there were garden sheds to put them in.'

'But then . . . why do they need you?'

'Well, for starters there's more energy in someone

like me than in a tree or a rock.'

'You mean they're feeding on us?' Alex glanced down at his hand in alarm.

'Don't worry, it doesn't harm you. It's not like they'll bite your arm off or anything.'

Alex heard a giggle inside his head and sent the *jinn* a thought of his own. *Behave, you.* The distinct image of a hungry tiger came back in return.

Mr Olmos was looking at him with a sideways sort of smile. 'There are dangers, Alex,' he said.

'What kind of dangers?'

'These young *jinn* are powerful creatures. And where you have power you will always find people trying to corrupt it.'

'How do you mean?'

The old man's face darkened and Alex saw storm-cloud memories brewing behind his black eyes. 'Too many *jinn* have been taken by people with bad intentions over the years. It won't happen to these three. It *won't.*' He spat the word like a bullet.

'I won't let it either. I won't let anything happen to Sally.'

Mr Olmos gaped. 'Who on earth is *Sally*?'

Alex grinned. 'Well, I've got to call her something. Until she picks her own name.'

'That's the most ridiculous thing I ever heard! Absolutely the most ridiculous and idiotic thing that I have ever had the misfortune to come across in my life.

And you, Alex Warner, are a ridiculous and idiotic child.'

'Shh, Mr Olmos,' Alex laughed. 'You're upsetting Sally.'

An icy wind swept away the last few scraps of summer. The October sky turned to slate. Starlings plucked whatever they could from the wet ground, preparing for worse to come.

'You're late,' Mr Olmos barked, as Alex arrived on the Thursday evening.

'I had to stay behind after school,' he replied.

'I thought as much. You are a very badly behaved young man. Nothing but a ruffian. Your teachers are right to punish you.'

'I was helping tidy up after an event. Not in trouble – helping.'

Mr Olmos frowned, as if such a thing was highly doubtful.

'How's Napoleon?' Alex asked him.

'What do you mean?'

'I thought you were going to spend the day reading all those books,' he said.

'Napoleon?' Mr Olmos waved his hand as if wafting away a bad smell. 'I know everything I need to know about Napoleon.'

'And what's that?'

'Napoleon was a very, very annoying little man.'

'That's it?'

'What else do you need? All these *books*. All these *words* going on about this and that. He was a small, selfish man who got lots of other people killed instead of doing something useful with his time.'

'So, what have you been doing?'

'Making butter.'

'Your churn turned up!'

'Never trust the post office, Alex. If I've learnt anything in life, I've learnt that.'

Alex thought that Mr Olmos must have learnt an awful lot more than that – after all, he kept genies in his shed – but kept his mouth shut.

'I've already brought them in,' said Mr Olmos as they entered the kitchen. Two of the *jinn* stirred, rising into the air in brief greeting and then settling back down on the counter. Sally buzzed towards Alex and he allowed their minds to connect. Once again that moment of overwhelming change, and then they were a pair. He felt like a master painter with a brush, creating whatever came into his head. Only it was a brush that had its own ideas, that would add in details and richness he never could have imagined. Was this how his mother felt when she worked?

'Can I take her outside?'

A scratching sound as Mr Olmos rubbed at his beard. 'I'd prefer you didn't.'

Sally flared slightly.

'See?' Alex said. 'She wants to. *You* let them out.'

'She'll stay low?'

Alex made the 'scout's honour' sign. 'You can trust me.'

He stepped into the garden, refastening the top button of his coat as he went. A security light flicked on. The anticipation was a living thing that squirmed inside him. It was the same feeling he got when doing his magic tricks, only sharper and more potent.

Mr Olmos's lawn was screened from the road by the fence on one side and from the neighbours by tall trees on the other. As long as the *jinn* stayed fairly close to the ground they were all but invisible to any prying eyes.

'Right then,' Alex whispered, 'let's see what we can do.'

Despite being reminded that the three of them were no more than toddlers, Alex was constantly amazed by the *jinn*'s abilities. Mirroring the pictures in his head was the least of it. He and Sally had spent the previous evening levitating a cup and saucer and flying it around Mr Olmos's living room. The old man had been impressed by this latest development right up until the point Alex had got too excited and the crockery had smashed into the wall, leaving a nasty tea stain on the paintwork.

Now Sally sensed his thoughts almost without him having to send them. She floated over to a rose bush – shrivelled and shuttered for the winter. She spread across it, wrapping each twig and leaf in a soft fire until the whole plant glowed. As Alex pictured the flowers,

Sally sketched their shapes and they came alive in flame, blooming from every branch. Now for the hard bit. Alex concentrated. Something other than his mind was at work, he knew. Something that was speaking directly to the *ifrit* on a level he couldn't understand. Her colour changed, sliding from orange-red towards white. She didn't burn brighter, but there was something more intense than normal and the light was too bright to look at. All of a sudden, she released the rose bush and zipped back to Alex's side.

He looked. There, where she'd drawn them a moment ago, actual roses – red, pink and yellow – adorned the branches.

'Nice work,' he gasped, and a delighted kind of laughter came back to him. A moment later though, the flowers began to crumble and dissolve like icing sugar. Soon there was nothing left of them at all. Alex felt a stab of frustration. *Next time*, he thought. *Next time we'll do better.*

His eyes landed on a small pot tucked away in the corner of the garden. He glanced back at the kitchen window. Mr Olmos was making his awful tea, paying no attention to them. The plant was a sorry-looking thing, no more than a short trunk and some ratty-looking branches. Not exactly the old man's pride and joy.

'Let's burn it,' he whispered. After all, if you had a living fireball to play with, it was only natural that at some point you'd want to blow something up.

He felt a scattered kind of energy from Sally and pushed the thought more firmly. *Do it.* He expected her to swoop on the tree then, to burn it to a crisp. He visualized it; pushed the picture from his mind to hers in that smooth, easy way that had become so natural between them. But then he realized that her chattering wasn't excitement at all. It was resistance. She didn't agree. She didn't want to.

'Come on,' he said. 'It's just a few twigs. I want to see if you can.'

But that wasn't quite true. Alex already knew full well that any of the *ifrit* could use their fire to destroy. He'd known it instinctively, and from the moment he bonded with them. He just needed to see it happen.

Burn it, he insisted and felt the *jinn* push back against him again. If their connection was like a perfectly smooth stretch of road then this was like a crease or pothole. Alex could feel the bump as he went over it.

Frustration crackled through him – a childish kind of temper tantrum that he wasn't getting his own way. He sent the thought once again, with far more force, and felt it take hold. Felt it overwhelm the spirit's resistance. Sally streaked forward and, in an instant, incinerated the pot plant. A brief rush of giddy pleasure rippled through Alex, leaving almost as soon as it came. He stared at the line of smoke twirling up into the night sky. Sally hovered a little way separate from him. A bitter taste in his mouth then, that swallowing wouldn't shift.

'What do you think you're doing?' Mr Olmos's voice was low, controlled and deadly. Alex turned to face coal-black eyes that burnt with anger.

'It was an accident,' he said.

'Was it now?'

'I lost control.'

'Don't lie to me.'

'Come on, it's just an old plant.'

'It was a living thing!' The shout came like a rifle crack, stopping Alex in his tracks. 'And besides,' Mr Olmos repeated more quietly. 'She didn't want to, did she?'

Dryness in Alex's throat. No words in his mouth.

'You must *never* force them,' said the old man. '*Never* push them. Never try to *control* them.'

'I didn't!'

It was nothing more than a thinning of the lips, but in that Alex could see the end of Mr Olmos's patience.

'All right,' he admitted. 'I did. But it was just a bit of fun. I didn't think it would . . . you know. I'm sorry.' He turned to Sally, who had come to rest on the path. *Sorry*, he told her, in a way that said more than the simple word ever could.

Mr Olmos softened a little and, at last, gave a single firm nod. 'I want to show you something,' he said.

17

Mr Olmos placed the book down in front of Alex. It was large, old and hand-drawn. The words weren't written in any language Alex could recognize. Even the letters themselves were strange.

'In English this book is called *The Locking and Unlocking of the Deepest Magics of Spirit Fire*,' Mr Olmos began. 'It's not a very snappy title.'

Alex nodded in agreement.

'But it tells a great many secrets, most of which will never now be deciphered. This page you're looking at contains a spell.'

Alex frowned. This was a lot to take in. 'What does it do?'

'It allows a sorcerer to take control of an *ifrit*. To trap them and force them to do whatever he or she wants.'

Alex ran his fingers over the parchment. The letters seemed to swim on the page.

'You know the stories of genies in their magic lamps?' Mr Olmos went on. 'Well, this is what it's like in real life. A magician performs this ritual and the spirit is tied to an object. They become a slave.'

'But . . . why?'

'You can't begin to imagine the power these spirits have. The things you've done with' – Mr Olmos swallowed in disgust – '*Sally*, are just the start of it. And remember, these three are just babies. A full-grown *ifrit* . . .' He sucked a breath through his teeth. 'A full-grown *ifrit* can be a terrifying thing. And in the wrong hands . . .'

Alex felt he was on a cliff edge, unsure whether or not he'd fall. 'Tell me,' he said.

Mr Olmos looked at him. Stared for so long that Alex wondered whether the old man would say anything at all. At last though, he dropped on to the sofa and began to speak.

'There is a story about a man,' he said, 'who lived many hundreds of years ago. He was a prince, who ruled over a small territory in my country. He was wealthy and powerful, but not nearly so much as he wished to be. He searched for many years, hunting down every clue until finally he came into possession of this book.'

The old man turned the page to a map, sketched in blue, black and red.

'He deciphered the ancient text and went into the Wadi Rum all alone.'

'The Wadi Rum?'

'A desert. At first there must have been villages, but those became fewer and farther between, until finally they were left behind altogether. Now there was just the desert and the pockmarked red mountains that rose up on either side. He travelled for days until he came to the Valley of the Moon. To the place where a *jinn* lived. The spirit had been there for thousands of years, they say, and it was strong. Stronger than almost any other.'

'What happened?'

'The *jinn* was powerful, yes, but also lazy and content. It had lived for so long it had forgotten how to be afraid. And so, when the man came, the spirit just laughed. It laughed as he read the words in the book and laughed as it felt a cold wind start to blow. But it stopped laughing when the spell took hold. When it found itself bound to the prince's staff. When it discovered that it was forced to do whatever the man told it to.'

A breath caught in Alex's chest. Sally was settled near him – a gently glowing cinder, comfortable again in his presence.

'I don't know how long the man had spent travelling to find the *jinn*, but to return home required nothing more than a word. The spirit was his to command. He forced it to raise a fortress from the desert floor, and he filled it with other men who craved power, and with dark things that wanted only madness. The sultan of that country sent an army against him, but the prince feared no army. He had his *ifrit* destroy them. Thousands of men burnt away to nothing in mere seconds. And after that, town after town, city after city, fell under his sway. And whatever kindness he might once have had in him was no more. They were hard times for the people. And hard times for the *jinn* he'd enslaved too, who was both pet and weapon.'

Mr Olmos stretched and went to the window.

'It wasn't enough though. The Sorcerer Prince wanted more and more. He made his spirit do awful things . . . things I will not mention. But in the end it came to nothing.'

'What do you mean?'

'The man, who now called himself a king, had made many enemies. One of them slipped poison into his drink one night. It weakened him just long enough for the *jinn* to break the spell. Free of the man, the spirit tore the fortress down and scattered all those greedy ones who had flocked there. The man begged for his life, but the *ifrit* was in no mood to be forgiving.'

'He died?'

Mr Olmos scratched at the back of his head. 'Perhaps. Perhaps not. The sorcerer was powerful. And the *ifrit* had granted him many powers of his own . . .'

'And the spirit?'

Mr Olmos shrugged. *Who knows?* 'But that's why. That's why you must never do what you did today. That kind of lust for power, for control, is an addiction. You mustn't let yourself be tempted.'

'But none of that's true, is it?' asked Alex. 'I mean, that's all just a story. Isn't it?'

'Probably,' Mr Olmos admitted. 'Some of it at least. But,' he said, turning to look at the infant *jinn* slumbering away near a pile of books about Napoleon, 'you of all people know now that there's truth in it. You of all people, Alex, know that *some* magic is real.'

18

The phone was ringing when Alex stepped through the door.

'Hello?' he answered.

'With whom am I speaking?' said a male voice at the other end.

'That's a weird way to start a phone call.'

'I beg your pardon?' The voice was familiar somehow.

'I mean, you called me,' said Alex. 'Bit funny to call someone and then ask who they are, don't you think?' There was a pause. Alex had a mental image of a man's face turning purple with righteous fury. 'Hello?' he asked again.

'My name is James Donaldson, Secretary of the Magic Society. I'm wishing to speak with Alex Warner.

If he is *finally* home.'

Alex clamped one hand to his forehead. 'Oh, Mr Donaldson, you should have said!' He'd just insulted one of the judges for the national final! *Nice work, genius.*

There came a prolonged bout of coughing, as if the man were trying to dislodge something nasty from his throat. 'You're a very talented young man,' he said at last, voice dripping venom. 'Rough around the edges. But talented.'

Alex's face turned hot. 'Thank you, sir,' he crawled. 'It's such an honour to hear that from someone like you.'

Donaldson's voice thawed a touch. 'I have some good news for you, Mr Warner,' he said. 'Jack Kellar has requested a little time with each of our finalists before the big day. A kind of mentoring session, I suppose you could call it,' the man went on. 'To talk about the craft. To offer advice.'

'Just him and me?'

'Apparently so. A remarkable man, Mr Kellar. I take it you can be available this Saturday?'

'In London?'

'Well you don't suppose he's paying house calls, do you?'

Alex fought the urge to be sarcastic in return and instead simply took down the address of the theatre where Kellar's show was playing.

He couldn't believe it. He was going to meet his hero!

Alex dragged the table and chairs to the edge of the dining room and surveyed his home-made stage area. He'd gouged a scratch in one of the floorboards, he noticed, with creeping satisfaction. His dad would be annoyed about that.

But that wasn't the point! He was meeting Jack Kellar the day after tomorrow, and then there was the national final seven days after that! He'd assumed he could just use the routine from the heats. He had a few special things he'd been saving up, but the spine of the show would be basically the same. Now, though, he was gripped around the heart by vice-like panic.

None of it was good enough.

The thought was needle-sharp and painful. He tried to calm himself by shuffling a deck, but his hands shook so violently that the cards spilt on the floor. How could he talk to Jack Kellar? His victory in the heats, it was clear to him now, was nothing more than luck. Hadn't those other fourteen contestants been, frankly, terrible? He was the best of a bad bunch, and nothing more than that. One of them had dressed up as Neville Longbottom, for goodness sake! *Neville!* He was going to embarrass himself. *Humiliate* himself.

He needed something new. He needed something different. He needed something that would show the judges, show the great Jack Kellar, that he had what it took. He needed something that would get him out of this frozen house and away from Freddie Taylor. He needed something. But what?

And all at once the answer was obvious.

19

Unlocked. Of course the gate was unlocked.

Alex felt a flash of annoyance with Mr Olmos. If the old man spent less time arguing with the postman and more time thinking about security, then perhaps no one would be able to break in and steal the fire spirits he kept in his garden shed.

A little stab of shame then. But there was nothing else for it. There was no way Mr Olmos would just *let* him take them to *Young Magician of the Year*! And besides, it was frustrating, always having the old man looking over his shoulder. Alex thought of what he could achieve if he was left to his own devices. The magic he and his *jinn* could weave together. His skin crawled with the thrill of it.

Slowly now, don't make a sound. Shut the gate behind you and keep low. No one in the kitchen. Good.

He slid one hand into his coat pocket and closed it around the little leather case inside. Lock-picking was a must-have skill for any serious magician. Houdini, for example, would have himself placed in a straitjacket, chained and dropped into an enormous jar of water. He'd have to free himself before he ran out of air. Alex had never tried anything that dramatic, but after several years practice there wasn't a door in his house that could stand against him.

And then there had been Freddie's locker, of course. That had been laughably simple. He flushed hot-cold and goosebumps ran across his forearms. *The Incident.* If only he hadn't . . . Still, there was nothing he could do about that now.

He scampered to the shed and pulled the lock-picking set from his pocket. The padlock might have been big, but it certainly wasn't clever, and it took no more than a minute for him to trip the levers inside. It opened with a satisfying clunk.

A noise from behind. Mr Olmos appeared at the kitchen window. He carried a mug, and his face was screwed up in a mask of disgust. That awful tea. Bitter saliva rose in the back of Alex's throat at the thought of it. More importantly though, he was completely exposed. If Mr Olmos looked out of the window he couldn't miss the schoolboy crouching on his lawn.

Don't look, don't look, don't look, thought Alex. If only his magic skills extended to mind control. But then, perhaps they did, because after a minute Mr Olmos threw the dregs of his tea into the sink, gave the mug a wash and left the room.

Too close. Far, far too close. But he was still alive. Still in the game. In one fluid movement Alex opened the door, slipped inside and closed it behind him.

The lock on the chest was actually more difficult than the door had been. Full of little tricks and traps. His heart jackhammered, and his fingers grew slick with sweat. But what about Houdini in his jar? Panic would only have made things worse. The master magician would have had to keep utterly, perfectly calm. To work each lock in turn, always trusting his own skill, until he finally got free. But still, his lungs must have burnt.

Alex closed his eyes and forced himself to focus on the mechanics of the thing. It was tricky, but not impossible. No, far from it. In fact, if he just moved one lever *there*, and the other one just *here*, then . . .

It clicked open. He stared down at the three *jinn* inside.

As ever, he was swamped by a sense of unreality, as if he was looking at something that simply *could not be*.

He recognized Sally at once and she drifted towards him, nestling inside the collar of his coat. She was hiding herself from view, he realized. How did she know what he had in mind?

No one in the kitchen. The coast was clear. He locked the shed behind him and bolted for the street.

Alex made his way off the path and down into the brambles and briars. The sky was ash-grey, but there was just enough light to see by. A delinquent fog hung in the air and curled around his limbs as he walked. He'd never been in The Wick this late before and found himself jumping at every rustle in the undergrowth. The place reeked of soaking leaves and moss. The trees were ancient monsters, each with hundreds of fingers that probed and searched in the gloaming. Only the warmth of the *jinn* tucked inside his coat stopped Alex from turning to run. It was like a second heart, beating in sync with his own.

He pushed through to the clearing where the Lightning Tree stood. In the half-light it seemed some twisted devil. Still, this was a place where Alex could be sure he wouldn't be seen.

He opened his coat and the *ifrit* came out. She swept over to the old tree and circled it a few times, before darting back to Alex. Agitated. Excited.

He'd spent the whole day and night thinking about how he could incorporate the creature into his act. He'd considered turning the genie into a giant flaming playing card, but that was just another version of the same old tricks he was trying to get away from. In the end, he decided that he'd use her to illustrate a story. A kind of magical animation, all drawn in fire. An illusion – or so people would think – just like Jack Kellar's Shadow World.

Alex linked his mind with Sally, feeling the now-familiar sense of falling and settling. He knew just the tale to use. *Hansel and Gretel.* She'd create everything in wonderful detail – the deep, dark forest, the two children leaving a trail of breadcrumbs to find their way back, the witch's house, the cage, the oven, the escape. It was perfect. The audience wouldn't know what had hit them.

But as soon as he began, he felt the spirit pull against him, as if she had a different idea. Remembering Mr Olmos's lecture, Alex made sure not to force his own thoughts on her. Instead, he waited to see what Sally would do.

She drew closer. Not in a physical sense, but somehow inside his head, as if she was tightening the grip they had on one another. He didn't fight it and felt her thoughts swarm in and around his. She had a story of her own, it seemed.

She changed in front of him, melting into the image of a desert valley. But he wasn't just *seeing* the story. It was almost as if it was being narrated to him, without language, but in some way that he instinctively understood.

*

A deep desert, criss-crossed with canyons and ravines. As the sun falls it lights up thin streaks of cloud and makes the parched landscape glow ghostly purple. A heavily laden train of people and animals pick their way through a half-lit maze of gorges, looking for the place where they will rest. The horses have bright, curious eyes; their flanks are heaving and slick with sweat. The air is thick with the smell of them. The caravan pauses. A fire is lit, food is cooked. Low, comfortable conversation. Laughter. Stars shine from a pure black sky.

The travellers know where they are. They have come this way and back again for their whole lives, and for the lives of their mothers and fathers before them. But still, they don't really understand the place. They don't realize how thin the cliff behind them is, and what lies beyond. And in the morning, they depart, taking their goods and animals with them. And it is only once they are gone that another figure approaches.

He is dressed like a man, but he is not a man. That much is clear from his eyes, which burn with deep flame. And also, if you look, you'll see that his feet don't touch the ground. He glides towards the place and, when he arrives, the rock parts for him, like a front door being swung open to welcome a visitor. He goes through into a natural plaza, completely encircled by cliffs. It is a perfect circle, as if someone had sliced a huge cylindrical core from the rock. The creature, whatever it may be, goes towards a clutch of glinting objects that lie at the centre of the chamber. He holds his hand out, and they float up into the air, coming to rest on his outstretched palm. There are three of them – perfect, black spheres, like obsidian marbles. They are warm to the touch and shine as if lit from a fire inside.

Alex jolted away. 'You!' he said. 'Those marbles were . . . You're trying to tell me all about you! Did all that actually happen then? Is that how you were *born*?'

He felt Sally tug at him, trying to pull him back into the story, but Alex's mind was too full of questions now to focus. He hopped from one foot to the other. It had been incredible! Effortless. The caravan, the stranger . . . every image had been movie-perfect. This would be his act! If that didn't win him *Young Magician of the Year* then nothing would!

He slumped down against the tree. The ridiculousness of the whole idea swamped him. What was he thinking? You couldn't do real magic on stage and just hope no one would notice! He and Sally would probably get locked up in a cage and examined by the government. No, it had been pointless taking her. He could never show people their *actual* power. He'd have to think of something else.

It was almost dark. He only hoped he could get the *jinn* back in the shed without arousing Mr Olmos's suspicion. But Alex had gone only a few steps back towards the main path before he noticed a figure, just on edge of the clearing. Someone had been watching him.

'What are you doing?' said Freddie, stepping out of the shadows. 'What *was* that?'

His heart dropped like a stone. No words came. If the *ifrit* had been seen, then what *could* he say? That it was a trick of the light?

Freddie stared, eyes wide. 'You . . . you *freak*!' The words were spat more than said. 'I knew you'd got weird, but I didn't know—'

'You can't tell anyone,' said Alex. 'I'm not messing around, Freddie; you really can't tell anyone about this.'

'What is it? What is that thing?'

Alex shook his head.

'Let me see.' Freddie took a step forward and Alex felt the *jinn* pulse rapidly inside the folds of his coat.

'Don't come any closer,' he said.

'I want to see it,' Freddie replied.

'You can't.'

'And you're going to stop me, are you?'

Freddie lunged at him across the clearing without hesitation. Alex stumbled backwards, tripping over a tree root and sprawling on the ground. But then, as if in slow motion, Sally moved forward. She rose up into the air, swelling to the size of a football, and there was a terrible sound inside Alex's head like the roaring of a forest fire. Freddie's eyes went wide with terror and even Alex had to scrabble back from the intense heat. He was still linked to her and knew at once with absolute certainty what she was about to do. She didn't care about anything but protecting them both.

'Stop!' he bellowed. 'Don't!'

He'd only uttered two words but so much more passed between them in that moment: ideas and signals that Alex couldn't even understand with his waking mind. But whatever it was worked, because a few seconds later the awful heat faded and the spirit floated back to his side.

Freddie cowered against the trunk of the Lightning Tree; body shaking, almost spasming. 'I hate you!' It was a scream of pure rage. 'She's going to send me to another school because of you! I won't know anyone! Because of you!' Flecks of spittle clung to his old friend's chin. 'I'm going to make you regret this, Warner. I'm going to make you pay.'

Alex ran, but the words echoed in his head and all the way into his dreams.

20

Sleep came down like a crushing weight. The new magic he'd explored with Sally – and the effort of stopping her from toasting Freddie – had drawn every last bit of energy from him.

And so Alex woke the next morning to find he'd slept right through his alarm. And not just by a little. His eyes went wide. He grabbed his phone, shaking it as if that would make a difference. He'd meant to get up by seven and it was already eight thirty. How could he have overslept; today of all days?

Idiot! You're meeting Jack Kellar!

An Alex-shaped tornado tore through the house, leaving chaos in its wake. In and out of the shower in one minute flat. Into his clothes before even properly dry. Hair styled with one hand while the other brushed his teeth. And finally, his bag, filled up with whatever he could see that might be useful – playing cards, a length of knotted ribbon, matches, and a couple of worryingly soft bananas in place of breakfast.

He could still make it. If he ran to the station at full pelt he could get the five past nine train; could still make it to the theatre by ten; could still take his chance to impress Kellar.

But there was something else, wasn't there? Something he was missing. He stood in his room, rucksack over his shoulder, with half of his brain screaming *GO!* while the other half begged patience. What was it? What had he forgotten?

A small movement in the corner of his eye. A light.

He turned towards it and, from the pile of clothes he'd tossed aside before climbing into bed, rose Sally.

'Oh, you've got to be kidding me,' he said.

Why hadn't he taken her straight back to Mr Olmos's house? In all the chaos of his encounter with Freddie, he'd somehow just forgotten. No, not forgotten. He'd been scared and drained, with no thought of anything but getting home.

He couldn't do both, he realized. Couldn't return her *and* make his meeting with Kellar. So what to do?

Alex opened the bag and the *jinn* came to nestle inside, without being asked. He smiled. She agreed with his decision, at least. They were in it together.

Run. Every second counts.

Finally, Alex careened around the corner and on to Station Way. The train pulled into the platform just as the machine spat out his tickets and then it was a straight sprint over the footbridge to Platform Three.

Beep beep beep beep, sang the train doors in warning. Alex tried to take the final few steps in one leap but lost his footing and tumbled forward. The concrete step rushed towards his face and he had just enough time to close his eyes . . .

But the crunch never came. Instead, there was a feeling of deep, enveloping warmth as a cushion of air scooped him up and put him back on his feet. He leapt – a headlong dive – and made it through the closing doors, coming to a rest in an undignified heap on the carriage floor.

Thank you, he thought, and felt Sally – resting inside his bag – signal back with the image of an enormous flaming thumbs up.

He made his way to the theatre, cutting through Trafalgar Square. Gusts of wind sent leaves waltzing across the paving stones, while rafts of broken cloud scudded through the sky above. A huge poster hung outside. The words *Jack Kellar's Shadow World* were written in silver against a storm-black background.

Leaning on the wall outside, staring into space,

was the biggest man Alex had ever seen. His enormous slab of a head was balanced on an ox's neck. The buttonholes of his shirt had been stretched so far that diamonds of hairy belly peeked through. Alex paused for half a second. Did he know the man from somewhere?

He made his way around the corner to the stage door as James Donaldson had instructed. A girl in black jeans and T-shirt asked him to write his name on a list and then showed him the way through to the auditorium. Following her through the labyrinth of worn corridors, Alex felt butterflies swirl and flutter inside him.

And then he was on the stage.

He'd thought the theatre where *Young Magician of the Year* was taking place was grand. How wrong could he be? This one was twice the size and three times as ornate. The stalls were a hillside of red velvet stretching away to the back of the room, whilst two tiers of seating loomed down from impossible heights. There were people everywhere, putting together Kellar's new show. The space rang with the sound of hammers. A sharp scent of sawdust. Alex felt like a fixed point in a whirl of movement. His heart pounded. This was where he was supposed to be. This was where he belonged.

The girl's fingertips grazed his shoulder. He turned and then, for some reason, blushed bright red.

'Over there,' she said, pointing.

Alex glanced across towards a group of people, most dressed in rough jeans, boots and T-shirts, who were leaning over a table with something laid out on it. It was a huge sheet of paper, he saw; the plans for the set they were building.

'Jack,' called the girl, and one of the men turned towards them. All at once, and for a worryingly long moment, Alex couldn't breathe. The man made his way towards them, crossing the stage in a few easy strides. There were flecks of paint in his hair that reminded Alex of the grey around his father's temples.

Kellar thrust out a hand. 'Great to see you again, Alex,' he said, in a voice that was loud without being harsh. 'Sorry about all the mess.' Whereas in his videos Kellar's smile seemed sly and knowing, face to face it was nothing but warm.

'Amazing job in the heats last week,' he went on. 'I mean, seriously, it blew me away.' Alex opened his mouth, but it was far too dry to produce any sounds. The magician jerked a thumb at the group behind him. 'I'm just getting in the way here. Let's find somewhere to talk, shall we?'

'We're different, aren't we?' said Kellar.

They sat amongst the stalls. Everyone else seemed very far away. To Alex it felt like it was just the two of them, haloed in the warm glow of a spotlight.

'You know what I mean by that? When I say

we're different?'

Alex thought he did.

'What do I mean?'

'You mean we know things no one else does.'

'That's right.'

Alex searched for more words. For the right words. 'You mean we think a different way to other people.'

'Exactly. *Exactly.*' Kellar clapped his hands together. 'Other people don't understand what it's like to practise a movement – the same movement – over and over again until it's just right. They don't understand that kind of dedication. It's not just that they can't, it's that they don't understand *why*. We're made differently to them.'

Alex was nodding along furiously now.

'Let me tell you something, Alex. I don't often tell people this but I'm telling you because I know I can trust you. At school, I was made fun of. Don't get me wrong, people asked me to show them magic. They were impressed. But for some reason card tricks aren't as cool as kicking a ball into a net.' He laughed, and Alex with him. 'And sometimes, when they made fun of me, it was all right. You know? It was something I could deal with. But other times it was *horrible*. And at times like those I just wanted to curl up into a ball. I wished I could make *myself* vanish, let alone a coin. I wanted to go far, far away . . . But you know what I never wanted to do?'

'What?' breathed Alex.

'I never wanted to stop. No matter what they said, or how they laughed, they never made me want to stop doing what I was doing. And lots of people do. Lots of people have a talent but they let themselves stop. We're different though, Alex, aren't we? We don't stop.'

'No, we don't.'

'I wasn't lying before. You're the real deal. Better than I was at your age. Don't stop. Don't stop for anything.'

'They laugh at me too.' Alex winced to hear the words out loud.

'Go on,' said Kellar.

A pause. He'd told no one else but his mum. Not Mr Olmos – though Alex thought he suspected something – and definitely not his dad. Still, he felt that Jack Kellar would understand. Hadn't he just said the two of them were different to other people? And didn't that mean that they were, in some way, the same as each other? Mr Olmos was a friend now, he supposed, but Jack Kellar was . . . well, he was Jack Kellar!

And so Alex told him about Freddie Taylor tearing up the pack of cards. He told him about the whispers that he was weird just because he didn't like the same things as everyone else. About the boys who delivered dead arms and rabbit punches when the teachers weren't looking. He even told him about the book he'd bought that his dad had never read. Through it all

Kellar only nodded, but Alex felt talking this way was the most natural thing in the world.

'Tell me about your act,' Kellar asked, when Alex was finished.

He glanced down. The velvety cloth of his armrest was almost worn through in patches, he noticed, revealing the padding underneath. 'I need to make some changes,' he said.

'I thought what you did was great.'

'But it's not good enough.'

'I get that. It's not about the competition, is it?'

Alex looked up. 'What do you mean?'

'I'm saying you might or might not win. The others are good too. So, you might or might not win. But that's not the important thing, is it?'

Alex shook his head.

'No,' Kellar went on. 'What matters is that it's good enough for *you*. That's got nothing to do with anyone else. You're the only judge that matters.'

'I just think my stuff's all so ordinary.'

Kellar gave a low chuckle, that for a half-second Alex found slightly unsettling. 'You're anything but ordinary,' he said. 'But, tell me, what have you got up your sleeve for the final. Pardon the pun.'

What could Alex say? *Well, Jack, I've discovered I have the natural ability to bond with powerful fire spirits. Just baby ones, but not bad, hey? I thought I might bring them along for the ride.*

Kellar must have misunderstood the silence because he put his hands up. 'Don't want to say? I respect that.'

He couldn't. Could he?

Alex thought of the shadow world he had seen Kellar perform. It was just a trick, but while watching he'd been convinced that it might – *just might* – be real. What if the same thing could happen in reverse? What if he could perform real magic, right here and now, and have Kellar think it was some incredibly clever trick.

His heart pounded against his ribcage. He was light-headed. Dizzy.

Alex reached down into his bag and pulled the jinn out. *Don't let me down*, he thought. She was quiet and still – looking like nothing more than a small, dark chunk of rock.

'OK,' said Kellar, 'you've got my attention.'

'This rock was found in the deepest depths of the Wadi Rum desert,' Alex began, but stopped short. Why spoil it with cheesy patter?

'Go on,' said the older magician.

'Well, let me show you,' Alex replied.

He cupped the *ifrit* in his hand and blew gently, whilst at the same time linking his mind with hers. She flickered, like a log fire coaxed back to life.

He could do anything, he realized, with a start. He could send fiery dragons racing above the seats. He could make fireworks burst in the gods. He could fill

127

the whole theatre with flames or burn it to the ground even. And everything would give the game away. It had to be small. Something Kellar would believe was just a trick. So instead he made the jinn rise slowly upwards and float about ten centimetres above his palm. She began to spin on the spot, like a gyro. The rotation grew faster and her light grew brighter until, at last, Kellar had to turn away and shield his eyes.

When he looked back, the light was gone. Alex had palmed the jinn into his pocket, leaving nothing but a faint smell of burning.

Kellar looked at him, mouth open. And then a smile; wider and wider. His hands came together in a firm clap. Again and again.

'Hell of a trick,' he said, gripping Alex's shoulder. 'And you're a hell of a magician. You came up with that yourself?'

'Well, I got the idea from my friend.'

'Friend?'

'Mr Olmos.'

'Unusual name. Don't get too many Olmoses to the pound. He's a neighbour, is he?'

'He lives in my town.'

'And what town's that?'

'Hatford Cross.'

'Hatford Cross . . . Got it.'

'Jack? You got a minute?' Someone was calling from the stage. Kellar sighed and stood. 'Well, I'll be seeing you next weekend then, won't I?' he said, standing and thrusting out a hand. 'And it's like I said, you're the only judge that matters.'

'It's been a real honour meeting you, Mr Kellar.'

That smirk again. 'Call me Jack,' he said. 'Now, have to go. Lots to do. Big rehearsal tomorrow!'

The girl had vanished from the stage door reception, so Alex signed himself out and emerged, blinking, into the daylight. The traffic seemed unreal, somehow. He was shocked, looking at his watch, to discover that he'd been with Jack Kellar for more than an hour. It had felt like five minutes.

The big man he'd noticed earlier was still leaning on the outside of the building. He glanced over at Alex but then his phone beeped, and he looked down, attention captured by whatever message was there. He pushed himself off the wall and, with a surprising turn of pace, started away.

Alex's own phone buzzed then: his dad asking where he was. The thought of their empty house loomed too high and too dark in his mind, and so he turned back towards Trafalgar Square. The train could wait awhile. It could all wait.

21

The hours slipped by and it was getting dark by the time Alex finally came to number thirty-three, ready to put the *jinn* back where she belonged.

The front door was open, swinging back and forth in the breeze.

'Mr Olmos?' he said warily.

No answer.

The hall was dim, and it took a moment for his eyes to adjust, but when they did he was greeted by a sight of utter chaos. All of his friend's things, usually so neatly ordered, were strewn across the floor. Boxes had been overturned and their contents shaken out on to the carpet. The rocket blueprints had been torn from the wall and lay crumpled in a corner. Mr Olmos's flamenco guitar was smashed into matchsticks.

Alex followed the trail of devastation into the lounge, already knowing what he would find. Sure enough, every book had been flung off the shelves to reveal the bare wood behind. The model railway wasn't in too bad shape, but the stationhouse lay in ruins, as if hit by a tornado.

The kitchen cupboards had been emptied. Their contents littered the floor. Alex saw the tea-mix there, mingled with uncooked rice and pasta. Vases had been smashed and plants torn from their pots. There was a rich smell in the air, which for a while he couldn't place. Then he saw a tray of spices overturned in the corner. The jars had cracked, leaking cumin and coriander. The back door was splintered and cracked along one edge. *Kicked in*, he thought.

The fog in his mind cleared as if blown by a sudden gust of wind. The house hadn't merely been smashed up. It had been ransacked. That meant someone had been looking for something. *They came for the jinn.*

He found the old man in the garden, slumped against the outside wall of the shed, his head buried in his hands. Alex dashed over, almost losing his balance on the slippery path. 'Mr Olmos!' he panted. 'What's going on?'

Alex stopped short. The man looked *old*, he thought. Of course, he knew that his friend wasn't a young man. He had wrinkles on his wrinkles, frizzy grey hair, and his hands were dappled with dark spots. For the first time though, Alex thought how frail he looked. How defeated. All the manic energy which seemed to animate his movements had been drawn off.

'Someone broke in?' Alex asked, squatting down on to his haunches.

Mr Olmos looked back at him through hollow, bruised eyes and gave the smallest nod of his head.

'Gone,' he said in a paper-dry voice. 'Gone, Alex.'

'You mean . . .' He swallowed. 'Do you mean all of them?'

'No, just one. But it doesn't matter. One's enough.'

There was a dizzying rush of guilt; sour and awful. Nothing to do now but tell the truth. Alex sat and drew his knees up to his chin, not caring how the wet grass soaked through the seat of his trousers. He reached into his bag and carefully drew out the slumbering jinn.

Mr Olmos's eyes went wide. 'I don't understand,' he said. 'How?'

A boiled-egg lump rose in Alex's throat. His face grew hot and he found he couldn't raise his eyes from the floor.

'I took her,' he said, at last.

He expected anger. He expected fireworks. He expected Mr Olmos to rant and rave and maybe even throw a few things around. But instead he got a very quiet, very simple response.

'For God's sake, why?'

'Because . . .' He didn't know, he realized. It had seemed so clear at the time. So right. But now he thought about it . . . 'Because I wanted to practise,' he offered limply.

'You can practise here. I told you that.'

'Alone, I mean.'

'Why?'

That question again. He forced himself to look the old man in the eye.

'Because . . .' *Because I wanted more, and I was scared you'd try and stop me if you saw.* He didn't need to say it out loud. Mr Olmos knew.

'I don't think you should come here any more, Alex.'

It was like someone had reached inside him and squeezed all his insides together. Not to see Sally again. Not to see *Mr Olmos* again. All at once there was the dull, sickening pain of having let someone down. Someone who had trusted him. Someone who had looked after him.

I'm sorry. He wanted to say it. He should say it. But there was something nasty crouching in the hollow that had formed inside him. Something that wouldn't let him admit he was wrong. So instead he slammed his hand on the ground.

'You're missing the point!' he cried.

Mr Olmos's eyes grew as sharp and hard as polished stone.

'I took her, OK, but I didn't do all this. I didn't break

in and smash up your house. Was anything taken?'

'No.'

'Then whoever did this must have been looking for the *jinn*. Don't you get it? The important thing isn't me, it's them.'

'Is that right?' The words were a coiled snake.

'That's right!' Alex went on, not even thinking now. 'That's right, and I know who it was.'

'And who's that?'

'Freddie!'

'Freddie?'

'From school!'

'You're telling me a twelve-year-old boy kicked my door down, trashed my things and then vanished?'

'What do you mean, boy?'

'We're talking about Freddie, aren't we?'

'Exactly. Freddie's a girl!'

Mr Olmos's mouth gaped. 'Hang on, Alex, you're telling me the boy who's been giving you all the hassle at school is actually a *girl*?'

'Of course. I thought you knew that.'

'Freddie?'

'Short for Frederica, of course!'

'What do you mean, of course?! You never even mentioned that!'

'Well, she's the one who did this. I know it.'

'You think this girl tried to steal three fire spirits?'

'Yes!'

'Don't be ridiculous.'

'I'm not. You don't know what she's like.'

'And how would she even have known they existed?'

'Because she saw Sally!'

Too late, he tried to stop himself.

'I see,' said Mr Olmos, his hands trembling a little.

'She saw,' Alex went on, 'when I was practising in The Wick. She saw me.'

Silence. Crackling, fizzing silence. A crow hopped along the garden fence, its beak darting this way and that.

It had been clear to Alex from the first time he saw Mr Olmos that the man liked to be angry. He enjoyed the fuss. It was his only true hobby, in fact, Alex thought – all the others were nothing but window dressing. But the anger that came now was nothing like he'd seen before. It wasn't exaggerated or a bit of fun. It was volcanic and primal and terrifying.

'All this time,' he growled, and Alex couldn't help but back away. 'All this time I've looked after them. Protected them.'

A heavy sickness in Alex's stomach.

'I trusted you,' Mr Olmos hissed. 'You – out of everyone! I thought there was something about you. Something different. Some kind of magic, even. So, I showed you. I showed you! And then you take her. You let someone *see*.'

'I'm sorry,' Alex tried.

'Sorry doesn't change it! Sorry doesn't make it better! You let someone else see them and now this happens!' One arm traced an arc towards the ruined house.

The old man's eyes blazed with fury. Flames flickered in those dark pools, as surely as on the tip of a match. Alex took a half step back, genuinely fearful. There was a held breath in which anything might be possible, but at last Mr Olmos simply slumped to the ground and buried his face in his hands.

'Go,' he whispered, with such tiredness and sorrow that it was all Alex could do to hold the tears back.

What could he say? What could he do to make it better?

'*Go*,' Mr Olmos repeated, still not looking up, and Alex knew he had no choice.

22

Paint peeled from the door and there was some kind of moss growing in the small glass panes above the knocker. Alex waited, poised on his back foot, and charged the moment it opened, barging his way past Freddie and into the hall.

'What are you doing?' she shouted, trying to pull him back by his sleeve. He heard the sound of fabric ripping and shrugged her off.

His mind was a whirl of furious static. The taste of blood was sharp and hot in his mouth, and a raging sea roared inside his ears.

His old friend stared, as if unable to believe he was being so bold. 'Get out of my house!' she cried.

'You did it,' Alex hissed.

'What are you talking about?'

'Mr Olmos!'

'Who's Mr Olmos?' Freddie pretended to look baffled, but Alex saw through it at once.

'You smashed all his things.'

'What are you talking about?'

'Last night. After The Wick. You found out where he lived, didn't you?'

'Last night I went home!'

'Liar!' Alex banged his fist on the wall, making a photo frame come loose and fall to the floor. 'You must have found out where he lived, and then you went there today.'

'I don't know what you're talking about,' said Freddie. 'Do you hear me?'

'You broke in.'

'I didn't break in to anywhere. I *wouldn't*. You've gone totally insane.'

Alex could barely look at her lying face. Any trace of the friend he'd once had was completely erased. The Freddie he'd known was brave to the point of stupidity but at least she was honest.

'Who else have you told?'

'No one!'

'Tell me the truth.'

'What was I going to say? That Alex Warner can do real magic. I'm not an idiot.'

'If you go round there again, you'll have me to deal

with,' said Alex. For one horrible moment, he thought Freddie might laugh. After all, hadn't Alex been running from her for months now? But she didn't. Instead, she looked frightened.

He pushed past her again.

'You're a freak, Alex!' Freddie shouted after him. 'I didn't tell anyone! Are you listening to me? I didn't do anything!'

But Alex was out and into the street.

23

'Where have you been?'

His dad marched down the hall towards him and Alex headed for the stairs without replying.

'I asked you a question,' his father said.

'I've been out.'

'Out where?'

'At Freddie's,' he snapped.

'I haven't seen you all day, Alex. Or yesterday!'

'I'm surprised you noticed.'

'I beg your pardon?'

'You could have sent me a message, Dad.'

'I did. Several.'

'I must have missed them.'

'I'd like to know what you've been up to, Al.' He ran a hand through his hair. 'Look, I've got to be out later, but—'

'I'm going upstairs.'

'No, you're not.'

'I'm tired.'

His dad flapped his arms in frustration. 'What happened to your clothes?' he asked.

Alex looked at his torn sleeve. 'Got caught on something,' he said.

'Caught on what?'

'I don't know, Dad, on something!'

'Have you been fighting?'

'No.'

'Are you in some kind of trouble?'

'No.'

'Tell me the truth.'

'Why are you so interested?'

'Because I'm your father!'

'You don't act like it!'

The shout echoed down the hall. Heavy, ugly silence fell. His father stared, and then slowly walked back into the kitchen. Alex watched him go, turned towards the stairs, and then changed his mind.

He let himself out again and walked back up the drive.

The temperature had fallen throughout the day and a thin, biting mist hung around. The twilight was sickly yellow. Alex pulled his coat tight around him.

He floated in a daze; buffeted one way and then the next. His mind churned through the events of the past few days – the competition, Jack Kellar, his father, *Mr Olmos* . . .

Something else was nagging too. Freddie's reaction . . . Alex knew her well. Knew her moods and her ways. Now that his blood had cooled it seemed to him that perhaps he'd been wrong. Perhaps she had been telling the truth after all.

It was all such a mess. How had the person he went to when things went wrong turned into his enemy? It was his fault, of course. That stupid stunt with her locker. His need to show off. Burning his bridges wherever he went. Well, the first thing was to make things right with Mr Olmos.

He knew as soon as he turned on to the road that the house was empty. No lights burnt in the windows, but there was something more than that too. An *absence*. He sprinted to the front door and pressed the doorbell. Nothing. He could feel the hollowness inside the house because it was the same inside his own chest. The *jinn* were gone, he thought. No, not thought: *knew*. Mr Olmos had taken them away. His hands hurt, and he realized he'd been digging his fingernails into his palms. He stared down at the crescent marks they'd made.

No.

It couldn't be.

Alex ran back down the path and around to the side gate, which was unlocked yet again. The shed looked normal from the outside, but as he approached he saw with a sinking heart that the padlock was undone. Inside, the chest was empty.

He fought back a wave of desperation. He needed to find them. All of them. He needed for everything to be all right again. For there to be someone in the world who didn't see him as a nuisance or worse. He slammed his fist down on to the table in frustration and closed his eyes at the instant explosion of pain.

But there, in the blackness behind his eyelids, something changed. It was as if he was looking at a street, but warped and changed as if seen through eyes that weren't at all human. It was Sally! She was nearby, he realized, just a few streets away. She was calling out to him, showing him where they were.

Alex began to run.

A hunched shape picked its way through the yellow fog.

'Mr Olmos,' Alex called, 'wait!'

The figure slowed a touch, allowing him to catch up.

'How did you find me?' The man's voice was tight.

'It's hard to explain,' Alex replied.

'Oh, I see. It was *her*, wasn't it? She called you.'

'I think so.'

'Well, it seems she's forgiven you, at least, then.'

'I'm sorry,' said Alex, and there was no deception in the words at all. He *was* sorry; really and truly.

Mr Olmos gave a sound that was somewhere between a cough and a grunt. His eyes were hard and sharp within the crinkled folds of flesh. At last though, he must have made his mind up, because as he turned away he beckoned for Alex to follow him.

'So where are we going?' Alex asked, keeping pace.

'Somewhere safe.' He jerked a thumb at the rucksack on his back. 'Somewhere to keep *them* safe.'

'Like a bunker?'

'No, not like a bunker. Where would I find a bunker?'

'I thought you might have built one. You know, as a hobby.'

'Are you taking the mickey?'

'No,' Alex lied.

Mr Olmos scowled. The fog cut off all sound but the padding of their feet.

'I've been thinking,' said Alex.

'Then we're all in trouble, aren't we?'

'I went straight home after you saw me. There's no way Freddie could have known where you lived.'

'Alex, I think my house was robbed by a dark sorcerer. One who wishes to use the *jinn*'s power for evil.'

'So, not Freddie then.'

'No, most likely not.'

'And if that happened? If a dark sorcerer did get hold of the *jinn*?'

'They'd draw down the young spirit's power until there was nothing left. Until they were blown away on the breeze.'

Alex sighed. 'OK, I don't think Freddie would be into that.'

'Why's this girl so unpleasant to you?'

'She's not. I mean, she *is*. For months now she's been . . .' All of a sudden, a lump in his throat. 'It doesn't matter. It's fine.'

'Alex, you stole one of the *jinn*, you put them all in danger, and because of you my house got smashed to pieces. I think you owe me one, don't you?' Mr Olmos glanced across, and then went on more softly, 'Besides, I think it would do you some good.'

Alex looked his feet, the flash of white trainers on black tarmac. Mist swirled around them. He could feel it at the back of his throat, damp as a forest floor.

'I'm an old man, you know,' said Mr Olmos. 'It would be nice if you started talking before I popped my clogs.'

'We were friends for ever,' Alex started, 'since the first day of nursery. Always together. And then . . . And then I messed up everything up.'

'What do you mean? I thought she was the one causing all the problems?

'Only because of what I did.'

A bat flitted overhead in search of insects. Mr Olmos said nothing, but his silence insisted that Alex go on.

'It was just a stupid joke,' he said. 'There's a boy in our year. Johnny Fish. Freddie told me that she liked him. You know what I mean?'

'I think I have some idea.'

'That she liked him, liked him.'

'And you were jealous?'

146

'What? No! I mean . . . no, she's my friend.'

'What happened?'

'It was only a bit of fun. And the others were telling me to go for it. I faked a Valentine's Card from Fish to Freddie and then I put it in her locker. She was over the moon when she read it. But when she told him that she . . .'

'That she liked him too.'

'Yeah. Of course, he knew nothing about it. Didn't take her long to realize it was all a set-up. And then she found out that I was part of it. That it was me that did it.' Alex let out a long, juddering breath. 'I tried to apologize. Told her it was just a joke. That she could get her own back any time. But she wouldn't speak to me. And then things just *changed*. It didn't happen all at once, but I realized she was talking about me behind my back.'

'Making up stories, you mean?'

'No, more like taking things I'd done or said and making them seem strange. Making people think I was different or creepy or something just because I'm into magic and all that. I didn't mind too much at first. But then her mates started making comments and pushing me and things. Started trying to corner me. It built up really slowly but one day I realized I was actually scared of her. Scared to come to school. She'd changed so much. Got so angry . . . and nothing I could say would make any difference.'

'I'm sorry,' said Mr Olmos. 'That's a horrible thing.'

'It's my fault though,' Alex insisted.

'People make mistakes, and other people forgive them. That's how it has to be. This Freddie girl shouldn't have done what she did either, Alex.'

The tightness in Alex's chest slackened, just a little. Some space was allowed to grow; something lighter to enter.

'But we're still no wiser about who robbed my house,' Mr Olmos said.

And just like that, Alex knew. *No way*, he thought. *He couldn't have.* But if not Freddie, then there was only one other possibility. Only one other person who had seen the *jinn*.

'What is it?' asked Mr Olmos.

Alex didn't reply. *It couldn't be him*, he thought. *Surely it couldn't be him.*

25

They left the town centre and turned on to Weston Road. The park lay off to their right, opposite a row of looming townhouses.

Mr Olmos kept checking behind, Alex noticed.

'What is it?' he asked.

'Probably nothing.'

Alex looked back. Was there someone there, obscured by the mist? A different sort of darkness, more solid in the gloom? He glanced over at his friend.

Mr Olmos shrugged. 'No law against having a walk,' he said.

'Not exactly the weather for it though,' Alex replied.

'It's probably nothing.'

But they stepped up their pace all the same.

Alex glanced behind once more, and saw the dark patch was a little further off. Whoever it was didn't seem to be following them after all.

And because he was looking behind he didn't see the enormous shadow emerge from a side road ahead of them. Not until it was far too late.

A monster came out of the darkness, quick and powerful, bringing with it the stench of sweat and decay. Grunts issued from its lumpen, misshapen head. It moved so swiftly that Alex had no time even to shout a warning before it swung one massive arm at Mr Olmos and sent him sprawling face first into the road. The rucksack containing the three *jinn* came off his shoulders and slumped at the kerbside.

The creature gurgled with pleasure. Mr Olmos rolled over, clutching the side of his head. He propped himself up on his elbows just as the shadow fell over him. Tendrils of fog, made yellow by the street light, swirled and eddied around the awful thing. It grabbed the old man by his collar, easily lifting him half in the air, and bent its face towards him as if sniffing its prey.

The sight of his friend lying there in the street snapped something inside Alex. Whatever force had been keeping him pinned to the spot vanished and he sprinted forward, parting the mist like a shark through water. The creature didn't see him coming and he shouldered into its side, hearing a satisfying crack followed by a bellow of pain.

But Alex was half the size of their attacker. With one dismissive swipe, the thing sent him reeling backwards into a heap. It lumbered towards him. And then, as its face was lit by a diagonal swathe of street light, he realized it wasn't a monster at all. It was an enormous man. A man he recognized. A man he'd seen before.

One meaty hand groped toward him.

'No!' someone shouted from a little way off, and then there was a long, high bellow.

No, thought Alex, not a bellow. *A war cry!* Just like the ones he and Freddie used to scream at imaginary enemies back in The Wick! There was the patter of feet hurtling over tarmac and then she emerged from the darkness, throwing her full weight into the man, catching him by surprise and knocking him sideways. She turned with snake-like speed to strike again – this time with a kick to his ribs.

The ogre moaned and rolled over.

'The bag!' shouted Alex, pointing to a crumpled shape a little way off.

She turned to him.

'Throw me the bag, Freddie!'

She tossed it over. He cradled its weight and could feel the *jinn* inside. Their thoughts came in waves. Fear and anger – potent as sea air.

'What's going on?' Freddie called, but there was no time to answer because their attacker had hauled his massive bulk up from the floor. Staggering, he made his way towards them.

Alex froze, rabbit-like, clutching the bag to his chest. The swaying beast seemed to move in slow motion.

'Alex?' asked Freddie. 'Don't you think we should—'

'Run! Take them!' shouted Mr Olmos, hauling himself up on to his feet. 'Don't just stand there! *Go!*'

The world rushed back to full speed, and Alex took off down the hill. The ground was soaking, but he knew he wouldn't stumble. Freddie's footsteps followed close behind, and beyond that a howl of frustration from the monster. The night swallowed them whole.

On they went, faster and faster, until Alex felt his lungs burn. Eventually, they came skidding to a halt. He looked around. They'd run clear past their school.

'Where are we going?' asked Freddie.

Alex realized he didn't know where Mr Olmos had been heading. Somewhere safe, he'd said. And now they'd outrun him for sure.

'Well?'

He stamped his foot in frustration. 'We'll have to lie low. Find Mr Olmos in the morning.' Without warning he found himself blinking back tears.

'Are you all right?' Freddie asked, panting.

He opened and closed his mouth a few times and then flung his arms around his old friend. At first it seemed as if Freddie would push him away, but then her muscles relaxed and the two of them stood locked together for a moment in the fog-choked night.

'How did you find us?' Alex asked.

'I was following you,' Freddie replied.

'Why?'

'I was going to beat you up, of course.'

'Thank God,' he said, laughing, and Freddie grinned back.

'Looks like someone did it for me though. Who was that?'

Alex didn't reply. But he knew the answer. He'd seen the man before. And he knew who he was working for.

26

A red carpet. People make their way down. They strike poses as photographers shout their names. Camera flashes like a lightning storm.

Beyond the barriers a crowd sways and rolls. Hands reach out to be touched. Phones capture the moment.

A man in a simple, dark suit comes into shot.

'Jack!' shouts someone. He turns to look and gives a wry little smile. He's embarrassed to be there, to be the centre of attention, but he knows the game and has deigned to play it. One hand tugs idly at his collar.

'Jack, can we have a word?' A woman in a blue dress comes into shot. She pushes a microphone under his nose.

'Katie, nice to see you,' he says.

'Quite a night, isn't it?' she replies, gesturing at the crowd, who whoop and cheer in return.

The man waves at them and turns back. 'Fantastic.' He smiles.

'Now, you've got a new show opening in a few months, haven't you?'

'That's right, Katie. It's called Jack Kellar – Shadow World.'

'And how's it looking?'

'We'll get there. Lots of hard work.'

The woman smiles at Jack and Jack smiles back at the woman.

Another man comes into view. A huge man. Where Jack is smooth, he is ungainly. Where Jack is handsome, he is repulsive. He looks like lumpy porridge poured into a tuxedo. He bends forward to whisper something in Kellar's ear.

'Him,' said Alex, pausing the video and jabbing one finger at his phone screen. 'That's who attacked us.'

'And you're sure about this?' asked Freddie. 'I didn't really see him properly.'

They were in her lounge, sunk side by side on a huge, threadbare sofa. Street light peeked round the sides of the curtains. The coffee table was strewn with plates of cake, biscuits and fruit. Agnes Taylor had been so over-joyed to see Alex after so long she had emptied the kitchen cupboards in welcome – especially when he told her he was allowed to stay over. Now the sound of her snoring wafted down the stairs, like the rapid bursts of a woodpecker at work. She'd never know they'd snuck downstairs.

'You're absolutely sure that's the same man?' Freddie asked again.

'Sure.'

'So, you're telling me Jack Kellar's bodyguard came all the way to Hatford Cross to steal your bag?'

'That's right.'

'Because the bag was full of fire spirits?'

'Yes.'

'Which your friend was keeping in his shed?'

'Yep.'

'And Kellar knows about these fire spirits because you showed him.'

Alex nodded.

'Because you were showing off.'

'I thought he'd think it was just a trick.'

Freddie plucked a biscuit from the table and stuffed the whole thing into her mouth. 'Way to go, genius,' she mumbled, spraying crumbs.

Alex gave an apologetic little shrug. 'Thanks for letting us come here,' he said, nodding towards the bag.

'Can I . . . can I see them?'

A breath caught in Alex's throat. *What harm can it do now?* he thought.

The *jinn* shifted listlessly around in the bag. Grieving

the loss of their protector. Freddie stared in wonder, slowly shaking her head.

Where was Mr Olmos? He'd told them to run, but Alex was starting to think that had been a very bad idea. He didn't have a number for him – didn't even know if he had a phone – and he couldn't connect with him in the same way he could with the Sally. All they could do was wait it out until morning and hope they could find him back at number thirty-three.

'And this is real?' asked Freddie, looking up from the bag.

'What do you mean?'

'I mean, you're not having me on? This isn't all some stupid joke?'

'Unfortunately not,' sighed Alex.

Freddie thought for a few moments. 'Awesome,' she said at last.

Later, then. The deepest part of the night. Even the snoring from upstairs had stopped. Everything was dark and smooth and velvet.

Bruises flowered across Alex's back and chest where Kellar's bodyguard had struck him. He sat on his hands so Freddie wouldn't notice them trembling. It did no good though. She didn't say anything, but he saw her glance down and register it. Without asking she made him a steaming cup of tea and when it had cooled a touch he drank it down in a few long gulps. His friend nodded her head in approval.

'Better?' she asked.

Alex looked at his fingers. Barely a wobble. 'Thank you,' he said.

They faced each other across the kitchen counter. A corner had broken away, revealing the chipboard underneath. Alex could see his own warped reflection in the blackness of the television on the wall. Eyes puffy, hair spiking out at the temples.

Freddie drummed her fingers. 'Won't your dad be wondering where you are?' she asked.

Alex breathed a noise of disgust.

'What, not at all?'

'Probably not even back himself.'

'Just because your mum's gone doesn't mean he can be a complete idiot all the time,' she said.

'He's not trying to be. He just doesn't notice stuff any more.'

'Like what?'

Like me, thought Alex, but kept that to himself. 'I think it's easier for him when he's working.' He snorted. 'But I did text him to say I was staying over,' he admitted.

'That's good,' Freddie said. Then, 'And how's your mum?'

Alex shrugged. 'She's amazing. But I don't want to . . . she's got enough going on.'

Freddie shook her head slowly. 'Grown-ups,' she said.

'Mr Olmos isn't so bad. You know he can play the drums? And apparently he's brilliant at darts.'

'Plus he has genies.'

'Yeah, that too.'

'It's stuffy in here.' Freddie went to the door, but Alex spoke before she could open it.

'I'm sorry,' he said.

No reply. Just the faint hiss of breathing.

'It was a stupid thing to do. The card, I mean.'

Freddie turned at last. Her mouth was drawn into a tight little line. 'Everyone laughed at me,' she said. 'Like I was the joke.'

'Yeah. I know the feeling.'

'I'm sorry too,' Freddie allowed. 'I probably shouldn't have had you beaten up.'

Alex grinned. 'You *tried* to have me beaten up. They never caught me, remember?'

'I could get them to have another go if you like.'

Alex went over and put his hand on her shoulder. Strange, how the tingles raced up his arm.

'Let's go outside,' she said.

The fog had lifted a little and Alex could make out hazy stars in the sky above. His skin grew thick with cold. A sudden image jumped to mind of a much younger Freddie, mud smeared across her face like war paint, charging through The Wick towards the alien hordes intent on taking over Hatford Cross. They'd never exactly established why aliens would be interested in their little town. But then, why not?

He looked across at his friend and, for the first time in months, felt no fear.

'So, magic's an actual thing then?' she asked.

'Looks like it.'

'And you're a real-life sorcerer.'

'That's what Mr Olmos says.'

'I bet you're not. I mean, I saw what you did at the Lightning Tree, but I reckon I could do it too.'

'Sure you could, Frederica.'

'You just wave your hands and around and boom. Magic.'

'That's it.'

'Abracadabra.'

'That's all there is to it.'

'I knew it,' she said.

Alex kicked gently at the wall. 'Is it true?' he asked. 'That you're being sent away?'

Freddie blew a strand of red hair away from her face. 'Mum was angry about the first call home from school. By the fifth one she'd had about enough.'

'So, we won't see each other?'

'Not much, no.'

'What if I talked to her?' Freddie shook her head, but Alex went on. 'Explained that it was my fault, that I provoked you.'

'Won't make a difference. Thinks the sun shines out,

when it comes to you.'

'It's the same for you and my dad. *How's Freddie? Is Freddie still playing football? When's the next game?*'

The night settled around them.

'So, when do you go?' Alex asked.

'Half term,' Freddie said. 'Three weeks.'

He let go a long breath. 'I'm sorry, Fred. Messing with your locker – it's all my fault.'

'No, not really. I wasn't exactly the golden girl before.'

Alex started to speak but she cut him off.

'Don't deny it. Remember the time they caught me stealing change from the canteen? Or when I told Mr Patel where to go?'

'But you were never sent away before.'

He looked across. Her eyes were glinting. Tears reflecting moonlight.

'I'm sorry too, Alex. For the things I said about you.'

'You're probably right, though. I mean, magic's not what most twelve-year-olds are into. I don't go out and kick a ball around or play around with computers. Not interested in cars or even films or things like that. I suppose I am a bit strange.'

'If you are then I am.'

She rested one hand on his and Alex realized there was no need for more apologies. Their feud had left scars but no blood.

He reached out to the *jinn*, inside their bag on the

kitchen counter. They were calmer now, but still on edge.

Don't worry, he told them, *I'm here. And you'll be back with Mr Olmos tomorrow. He'll take care of you. He'll make sure everything's all right.*

Alex slept fitfully and woke while it was still dark. Freddie was up early too, sneaking downstairs and bringing him an orange juice from the kitchen.

They were just draining their glasses when a shrill blast made him jump. His mobile was ringing. Unknown number.

Freddie raised an eyebrow. 'It's only six in the morning,' she whispered. 'On a Sunday . . .'

'Hello?' Alex said, answering, and holding the phone so Freddie could hear too.

At first there was nothing but breathing. Then a voice on the line.

'Would you like your friend back?' it said.

Cold fingers walked their way up the back of Alex's neck.

'Who is this?' he asked.

'Would you like your friend back?' the voice repeated.

'Where is he?'

'Doesn't matter where he is now. But tomorrow you can have him back, as long as you bring me that bag you took. And make sure everything that should be in

162

there *is* in there. The playground in Weston Park,' the voice went on, 'we'll be there at seven in the evening.'

'Is he . . .' Alex barely dared to ask. 'Is he all right?'

'He's seen better days, kid, that's for sure.'

The line went dead.

The two friends looked at each other.

'What are we going to do?' asked Alex.

27

How are you supposed to concentrate on school when you're waiting to ransom your friend back from a famous magician in exchange for three powerful and probably immortal fire spirits?

'Am I boring you, Mr Warner?' asked Mrs Mutola in third period.

'No, miss.'

'Then perhaps you'll answer the question.'

Alex glanced at Freddie, who just shrugged. 'What *was* the question, miss?'

She sighed, as if the world was nothing but a disappointment, and Alex most of all.

'See me after class,' she said.

Eventually, though, it was time. The evening sky was stained with dark clouds. Weston Park was empty, save for people in their work-clothes and trainers, cutting through on their way home from the station. Rucksacks over their shoulders with their smart shoes inside.

The playground was tucked away in one corner and reached by way of a winding path, flanked by conifers.

'You think they'll be here?' asked Freddie.

'Of course,' said Alex. *They have to be.*

The three *jinn* had spent the day in his locker at school. It had seemed safer than leaving them at Freddie's, where her mother might stumble across them. And besides, there were no actual rules against keeping magical creatures in your school bag. There were rules against burning the whole building down, of course, but that had been a risk he he'd been willing to take.

Alex felt sick and dizzy. This was all too hard. He had to get Mr Olmos back, that went without saying. But he couldn't give the *jinn* over either. So what was left? Using Sally against Kellar's bodyguard was impossible. He remembered the terrifying, scalding power she'd displayed when Freddie had threatened them. Alex couldn't control her well enough to be sure she wouldn't burn the man to a crisp, and he didn't want to end up a murderer. So, what then?

Alex glimpsed the figure up on the road, huge and

hulking against the darkening sky. With him was a smaller, crooked shape. They made their way down the path until they were facing Alex and Freddie across the playground. A roundabout, of all things, stood between the two sides.

Mr Olmos didn't look good. He was hunched over and leaning on his captor's arm for support. His jacket was torn, and his hair stuck up even more wildly than usual.

The ogre grinned a mouthful of yellow teeth. 'That it?' he asked, pointing one ham-sized hand at the rucksack.

'No,' said Freddie, before Alex could respond, 'that's the bag with our packed lunches in it.' She rolled her eyes. 'Of course that's it, you moron.'

Confusion on the bodyguard's face. Alex turned to Freddie in disbelief. She shrugged and gestured for him to get on with it.

'Are you all right, Mr Olmos?' he called.

The old man mumbled something under his breath.

'Mr Olmos?' Alex couldn't keep the tremor from his voice.

This time he looked up at the sound of his name, but his eyes were cloudy, and he didn't seem to see them properly. He hung his head again, murmuring to himself.

'What's wrong with him?' asked Freddie.

The ogre gave a low, gurgling chuckle. 'Talks a lot, your mate. Talks *all the time*. Gave him a little something to keep him quiet.'

'What do you mean, gave him something?' asked Alex.

'He means he's drugged,' said Freddie.

'Don't worry, kiddies,' the ogre laughed. 'He'll wake up properly in a few hours.' The smile became broader. 'As long as you hand the bag over, that is.'

Mr Olmos was still talking in a low, slurred voice. It was hard to make out, but seemed to be the same thing repeated again and again.

'*Ni-ma-te. Ni-ma-te. Ni-ma-te . . .*'

What was he trying to say? *Come on, Mr Olmos*, Alex thought. *Do something. Give me some idea how I'm meant to get us out of this!*

The old man just swayed, constantly whispering through broken lips. '*Ni-ma-te. Ni-ma-te. Ni-ma-te . . .*'

Alex could hear the *jinn* inside his head. They were asleep and dreaming of things so strange that no human could possibly understand. He could wake them. He could set them loose on this awful, grinning man. He could save Mr Olmos.

But he couldn't really, of course. Not without the risk of something terrible happening. He glanced across at Freddie, who glared at the ogre with ferocious intensity. She looked like a small warrior queen and Alex was glad beyond words that she was back on his side.

'Let him go,' he said at last. 'Let him go and I'll hand it over.'

The ogre shook his head. 'Bag first.'

'No deal,' said Freddie.

'No?'

'No.'

With one swift movement the huge man grabbed Mr Olmos by his collar and hoisted him into the air. He dangled there, legs kicking.

'Put him down!' Alex shouted, starting forward, but Freddie put an arm out to hold him back.

Mr Olmos struggled weakly while the man just grinned and grinned.

'There's other ways of keeping him quiet, you know,' he called.

'All right. All right!'

The ogre set Mr Olmos down but kept a firm grasp of his collar. 'Throw the bag over here,' he demanded.

Think of something, Alex. Think of something now.

But what was there to do? It was hopeless. The bag was heavy on his shoulder and rubbed his forearm as he slipped it off. A breath. And then he threw it, watched as it arced through the night and into the arms of their attacker.

'Now give him to us,' Freddie shouted.

The ogre smirked. 'I don't think so, kids,' he said, starting to pull the old man away with him. 'But nice to see you again.'

'No! You can't have them!' The shout came from Mr Olmos, who jerked so violently he almost tumbled on to the ground. His eyes had narrowed and sharpened. Veins stood out at his temples and on his neck.

'Quieten down, grandad,' the ogre said, leaning his granite skull in close to Mr Olmos's face. But he must have seen something there he didn't like or wasn't expecting because all of a sudden, he let go and sprang back, as if stung.

Alex stared at the ogre in puzzlement. The man's face was a mask of confusion, bleeding into fear. What on earth could have made this huge, swaggering monster change so suddenly?

'Alex,' said Freddie very quietly. 'What's happening?'

'What?'

'Look,' she hissed.

He turned his gaze to Mr Olmos, and his mouth fell open in amazement. His friend was *changing*.

His eyes burnt. It took Alex a few moments to register it – to believe it – but there was actual fire there. Red-black flames that flickered and danced in his skull. The old man drew himself up straight and the fire spread. It came from his fingers and rushed across his arms. His face was still familiar but wreathed in scorching orange light.

'Mr Olmos?' Alex called. 'Mr Olmos, what's happening?'

But he knew. He knew without being told. He could barely believe it was true, but just then he knew what Mr Olmos was. He stared at his friend. Human, still, but only just. Fire licked across his skin and there was a reek of sulphur in the air. Heat came off him in waves.

Kellar's bodyguard had seen enough. He ran. Mr Olmos took a few steps after him and flames began to swirl and gather around his right hand. He raised it, ready to throw a burning missile, but all at once stumbled and dropped to his knees. His fire sputtered and dimmed, as if suddenly robbed of oxygen, and he pitched forward, coming to rest face down.

Alex sprinted to him with Freddie just a step behind.

'Be careful,' she said, but Alex was already doing his best to roll him over.

'Help me,' he said, and with Freddie's assistance he managed to lever Mr Olmos on to his back. The fire was all but gone – no more than a few embers glowing in his eyes.

'What on earth was that?' Freddie asked.

'We need to get him home,' Alex replied. 'Him and—' He scanned around. The bag was gone. Alex slumped to the ground next to Mr Olmos. All the breath was gone from his lungs.

Gone.

Taken.

'What am I going to do?' he asked the night sky.

'We,' came the reply from Freddie. 'What are *we* going to do?'

28

They half dragged, half carried Mr Olmos home. Alex fished around in the old man's jacket pocket for the keys – fingers working through safety pins, matches, dice and a few random chess pieces – before he finally found them.

'God,' said Freddie, as they stepped into the hallway. 'Looks like a bomb went off in here.' She picked up an electric guitar, snapped at the neck. 'You didn't say he was a rock star.'

'He does a lot of things,' replied Alex, half-dazed. Sally was gone. *Gone.*

'Come on,' said Freddie, clapping him on the shoulder. 'Let's get him comfortable.'

Broken china crunched under the soles of their

shoes as they moved through into the living room.

Alex held Mr Olmos upright as Freddie cleared a space on the sofa. The cushions had been slashed open, he noticed now, and were spewing yellow foam. The ogre had been thorough in his search. They laid the old man down.

'I need some water,' Freddie said firmly.

Alex stared. Mr Olmos was badly hurt and the *jinn* taken by Kellar. *How did it get to this?* he thought. The question had an easy answer. Him. Alex Warner. It was all his fault. He tried to force down the lump in his throat.

'Alex?' said Freddie. Her face was very still and serious. 'Alex,' she repeated. 'No time for that. He needs you. Water. Now.'

He turned hot. Embarrassed for Freddie to see him cry. Embarrassed to be letting her down.

He filled a bowl from the hot tap and Freddie went to work cleaning the dried blood from Mr Olmos's face. Her movements were precise, her fingers long and slender.

'Can you shut that thing up,' she said, out of the blue.

Alex listened. Freddie was right. An irregular *tick*, *tick*, *tick* was coming from somewhere in the room. He searched around and discovered a half-smashed old clock on the windowsill. Its guts were hanging out, but the mechanism was struggling on in some kind of death-rattle. Alex looked at Freddie, who just shrugged back. With no other option, he bashed the clock down on the sideboard – once, twice, three times – silencing it for good.

A burning smell – acrid and strong. Their heads snapped round in unison. The tea towel, which Freddie was still holding to the cut on the side of Mr Olmos's face, had started to singe. Black spots bloomed all over, burning through into pound coin-sized holes. She leapt back and thrust the smouldering cloth into the bowl of water.

'What was *that*?' she asked sharply.

Alex reached for Mr Olmos's hand. Too hot to touch for more than a second. 'He's changing again . . .'

'Yeah, well, he's going to set light to the sofa.' Freddie began to back away.

'Mr Olmos? Mr Olmos!'

The old man stirred a little. '*A-ne-ma-te*,' he mumbled over and over again.

'Mr Olmos, can you hear me?' Alex repeated. 'You need to . . . I don't know what you need to do, but you need to do something. Can you hear me?'

The room filled with the lush smell of baking rocks.

'I'm serious,' Freddie said. 'If he doesn't stop this, the whole street's going to go up in flames.'

'He can't help it. He's not really awake. I don't think he even knows what's going on.'

'So, what do we do?'

'There must be some reason it's happening now.

Something he does to stay looking human. Something he couldn't do while he was kidnapped.'

'Well, what?'

'How should I know?'

The two of them stared helplessly at one another, while Mr Olmos kept muttering his nonsense words beside them. And then, in a rush, the answer came to Alex.

'I know what he's saying!' he shouted, leaping to his feet. '*A-ne-ma-te!* I know what it means!'

'And are you going to tell me?'

'I. Need. My. Tea!'

'I don't think now's the time for a cuppa, Alex!'

'Stay here!'

He sprinted to the kitchen. He scooped some of the spilt mixture from the floor into a mug and bounced from foot to foot as the kettle came to the boil achingly slowly.

'Alex!' called Freddie; her voice was filled with utter panic.

He carried the cup through but stopped dead at the door, gaping at the scene in front of him. Mr Olmos wasn't really Mr Olmos any more. His body had risen a metre from the sofa and burnt like a log fresh to the fire. There was something recognizably human there, but it was changing by the second. Ancient flame and power.

'You're sure about this?' Freddie said.

'I know what I'm doing,' he replied, coming forward. 'At least, I think I do . . .'

He raised the cup towards the fire. Pain seared through his arms and he pulled back. *Come on, Alex*, he thought. *Fast. Just be fast.*

He darted his hands forward as quickly as he could, tipping the cup towards Mr Olmos's mouth. Half of it missed, turning to steam, but some of it found its target. *Please be enough. Please be enough.*

'We've got to go, Alex,' said Freddie.

'I can't leave him.'

'I'm not messing around, we can't stay here.'

'It's my fault!' Alex took a deep breath. 'I have to stay. To see. You go.'

He turned back to Mr Olmos, but seconds later a hand joined with his. He turned to Freddie, who refused to meet his eye.

'Just so you know,' she said. 'I agree that this is all your fault.'

29

Mr Olmos woke up in a very bad mood.

The tea had worked its strange magic slowly – far too slowly for Alex's liking – but eventually the old man had reverted to his human shape. For a few hours he lay still, but it seemed a peaceful kind of sleep. Now though, that peace had been blown away by a thunderstorm.

'What do you mean, you handed them over?' he barked at Alex.

'What else did you want me to do?'

'How about *not* hand them over?'

'He was threatening you. I just told you, it was Jack Kellar's bodyguard. Jack Kellar's the one who wants the *jinn*. He had you by the collar, was almost throttling you!'

'So?'

'So, I was saving your life!'

'What did I tell you before, boy? I'm not the important one. The *jinn*! Keeping them safe! That's all that matters!'

'So I should have just left you?'

'Exactly!' Mr Olmos threw his hands in the air. 'That's why I told you to run!'

'Hang on a second,' Freddie butted in.

'Remind me who this person is again,' said Mr Olmos with a scowl.

'My name's Freddie. You know that, because I've already told you ten times.'

'Freddie is a boy's name.'

'And Mr Olmos is a stupid name.'

'Mr Olmos is a perfectly good name. I picked it myself!'

'Alex didn't have any choice.'

'He could have left me.' The old man slammed his hand on the table.

'And what would the baby genies have done without you?'

'What do you mean?'

'They need to *ascend*, right?'

'Right . . .'

'Well, Alex and I don't know how to do that, do we?'

'That's not the point,' Mr Olmos muttered, sounding less sure.

'No, the point is that you're being a complete idiot. Having a go at Alex, who basically saved your life, instead of thinking about what we do next!'

Mr Olmos snorted and rubbed a hand through his beard. 'I like this one, Alex,' he said at last. 'She can stay.'

Freddie rolled her eyes. The room fell into a squirming, uneasy silence.

'So,' said Alex conversationally, 'you're a genie then.'

'Looks that way, doesn't it?' Mr Olmos gave the kind of pout most often seen on the faces of grumpy toddlers.

'And the *jinn* in your shed,' Alex went on, 'they're your children?'

'It doesn't really work like that.'

'How does it work?'

'It's complicated.'

'Right, I see,' nodded Alex. 'But you're hiding in the shape of a person.'

'That's complicated too.'

'It's that tea you drink, isn't it? It's like a magic potion that keeps you human-shaped.'

Mr Olmos paused. 'OK, it's not that complicated.'

'But you live in Hatford Cross?'

'That's right.'

'I mean, you're a genie, and you live in Hatford Cross. *Hatford Cross.*'

'Can you stop saying *Hatford Cross*, please, Alex?'

'OK, but . . . *why?*'

Mr Olmos sighed. He looked normal. Alex searched his eyes for some trace or spark of fire, but there was nothing there.

'Why choose to live here?' he asked again.

'I've already told you,' Mr Olmos began, 'in a manner of speaking. You remember the story about the Sorcerer Prince?'

'The one who trapped a genie? Made him do his bidding? Destroy cities? Wait, that was—' Alex gaped. 'That was *you*?'

'I was under his control for a very long time. Longer than the lifetime of a normal man. I did many terrible things. He forced me to do them. When it was over, and I was free, I fled back to the desert. But I couldn't rest. I knew that eventually someone else would come. It might be hundreds of years, but eventually someone else like him would come, and I wouldn't be so fortunate again. For a long time I waited, though. And then . . .'

'And then you decided to move to a semi-detached house in England,' Freddie offered. Alex shushed her, and she made a rude gesture in return.

'I found the three young *ifrit*,' Mr Olmos said. 'I could sense them. There are secret places where *jinn* are born into this world, you see. I found them when they weren't even hatched. Just three black stones—'

'Like marbles full of fire,' Alex finished.

Mr Olmos tilted his head. 'How do you know that?'

'Sally showed me. When I took her to The Wick. I think she showed me what happened when you found them.'

'Who's Sally?' Freddie asked.

'One of the *ifrit*,' Alex replied.

'You named it *Sally*?'

'Now's not the time, Fred.'

'I agree with the Freddie-girl,' Mr Olmos said. 'Sally is a stupid name for a fire spirit.'

'Can we get back to the subject?' Alex snapped.

Mr Olmos sighed. 'I gathered them up and left. Gathered the ingredients I needed for my tea; took this form you see now, and I went far away. Far, far away to a place where there was no desert, only green hills and gentle rain.'

'Hatford Cross.'

'It wasn't called that then. But yes.'

'And you've been looking after them ever since?'

'There's not long to go. It's almost time for their ascension.'

'If we can get them back, that is,' Freddie added.

'We will,' said Alex. 'We have to.'

Mr Olmos wobbled to his feet. 'What we need is a plan,' he said, 'and it just so happens that for a while researching military history was one of my hobbies. I've got a whole box of books in the attic about how to plan a campaign. I'll go and get them.'

'Great,' said Freddie. 'Let's start a book club instead

of doing something useful.'

'Well, what would you suggest?'

'I suggest we go to the police.'

'The police? And tell them what?'

'That you were kidnapped and robbed, for a start.'

'And when they ask what was stolen?'

'We make something up!'

'Will you two stop it!' Alex shouted. 'Honestly, you're like a couple of babies.'

Freddie and Mr Olmos both looked down.

'I know what we have to do.' He took a deep breath. 'Think about it. Kellar thinks we can't touch him. He thinks *no one* can touch him. He's not going to ground. He's still got a show to put on. Still got interviews and things to do. And he's still got a competition to judge.'

'A competition that you're invited to,' said Freddie.

'We know *exactly* where he's going to be on Saturday.'

For the first time since he woke up, Mr Olmos smiled. 'And that's our chance to get them back,' he said.

30

Alex closed his eyes and the world around him fell away. Not just the vaulting arches of St Pancras station, or Mr Olmos and Freddie beside him, but the events of the week as well.

He forgot about the sleepless, worried nights. He forgot about Freddie having a go at James Gilfoy and Samuel Down, telling them that if they ever messed with Alex again they'd be sorry. He forgot pleading with his teachers for them to put a good word in with Agnes Taylor so that his friend wouldn't be sent away after all. He even forgot about the lessons spent staring into space, imagining Jack Kellar learning to use the *jinn*'s power. Draining them. Hurting them.

He forgot and forgot, until the only memory left was

the fight he'd had with his father the night before.

'It's midnight!' his dad had shouted.

They'd been at Mr Olmos's house on Friday evening, going over and over the next day's plan. Time had gotten away from them.

'Well?' His father's face was tinged red. 'Did you hear me?'

'So what if it's midnight?'

'So, you're eleven years old!'

'I'm twelve, actually.'

'Where have you been?'

'With Freddie.'

'At Freddie's?'

'Yes.'

'Except I rang Agnes, who said she hadn't seen either of you.'

'I mean, we were at another friend's house.'

'And what friend is this?'

'You don't know them.'

'What's their name?'

'Why do you even care?' Alex couldn't help it.

'What did you say to me?'

'You're hardly here yourself.'

'I'm an adult.'

'So how do you know I'm not doing this all the time? How do you know I'm not wandering around town in the dark *all the time*? You're never here, Dad, so how would you know?' His words bounced off the iron radiator in short echoes.

His father's mouth hung open. Alex hadn't waited for a response, instead storming to his room, face burning.

'We'll talk about this in the morning,' his dad had shouted.

But they hadn't. Instead Alex had risen before the sun was up, dressed in his suit and tie, and gone to number thirty-three.

He concentrated. Forced himself to forget all that too. Slowly he felt it slip away.

And then he was suspended in the blackness, above a teeming city of lights. London. He found he could move around the space at will. It almost scared him, how quickly his power grew – scared him to think of what it could become.

Alex searched with his mind, hunting for those three points of fire. Hunting for Sally. And there she was, just where he'd hoped she'd be. Calling to him. Asking him to come. He opened his eyes and the world rushed back.

'We were right,' he said, turning to look at the tight, concerned faces of his friends. 'They're at the finals. At the theatre with Kellar.'

'Then what are we waiting for?' asked Freddie.

Mr Olmos shook his head and uttered a wet sound of disgust.

'What is it?' asked Alex.

'The arrogance of the man. Not even trying to hide them. Thinks he can do whatever he wants.'

Alex gritted his teeth. 'Well, let's go and prove him wrong then.'

31

It seemed to Alex that the noise rose like a storm. Through the haze of lights, he could make out his friends, on their feet, cheering. Had the other contestants got such big rounds of applause? It was hard to remember, but the thought struck him like a thunderbolt that he *might actually win*. A grin snaked its way across his face.

But then he glanced to the side, towards the judges' table, and remembered that the competition wasn't the important thing at all. James Donaldson stared back with watery eyes and pursed rubbery lips. Jack Kellar, on the other hand, was clapping enthusiastically, pausing only to scribble a few notes on the pad in front of him. He looked so casual, so natural, sitting there.

Alex felt a stab somewhere in the middle of his chest. He wanted Jack Kellar to tell him he was good. He wanted Jack Kellar to award him with the trophy. He wanted Jack Kellar to be the kind of person he'd always imagined him to be.

But he wasn't. The man was a thief. He hired thugs to beat up children and old men. He took what he wanted with no thought for anyone else. But still Alex wished he could go back to the week before, when he'd sat with him and felt as if, for once, he really, truly mattered.

He was outstaying his welcome. The applause had slackened just a touch. Alex turned and headed for the wings, giving his head a quick, livening shake as he went. The real business was about to begin.

A few people backstage offered their congratulations while some of the other contestants glared. Mr Olmos and Freddie were waiting for him in the now-packed foyer.

'Kellar and Donaldson are heading for a judging room up on the second floor,' Alex said. 'We've got twenty minutes before they announce the winner.'

'And you're sure,' asked Freddie, 'that the genies are here?'

'They're here. I can feel it. Let's get to his dressing room.'

'What if it's locked?'

'I can take care of that.'

A new voice cut across the room. 'Alex,' it said.

'Alex, wait!'

He turned.

It was his dad.

Anyone looking would have seen the resemblance. The same jaw, the same way of holding themselves, the same bright eyes. Now, though, those eyes were flaming with shock and anger.

'What are you doing here, Dad?' asked Alex, and his voice was sharp as a snake's hiss.

'You were gone when I got up.'

'So?'

'So, you're too young to be going off by yourself without anyone knowing where you are!'

'Mr Olmos knew.'

'And who on earth is Mr Olmos?'

Alex jerked a thumb in his direction. 'My friend.'

The boy's father looked across. Dark clouds of suspicion and fear scudded across his face.

'Mr Warner, if I can introduce myself,' Mr Olmos began, extending a hand, but the man ignored it.

'What kind of friend? Alex?'

'It's none of your business, Dad.'

'Of course it's my business. Freddie, maybe I'll get some sense out of you. What's going on here? Who is this man?'

'He's Alex's coach!' she blurted out.

'What do you mean, coach? Why does Alex need a coach?'

'For his magic!'

'That's right!' Mr Olmos added.

'Mr Olmos here is sort of a . . . a teacher,' Freddie went on. 'No, not a teacher. A . . . what's the word?'

'A mentor,' said Alex flatly. 'He's my mentor.'

Mr Olmos looked at the boy. The creases around his eyes deepened and he flushed with pleasure.

'And you've brought my son to London, have you?'

'If we could just talk, Mr Warner . . .'

Alex's father dismissed the suggestion with a wave of his hand. 'Sneaking off to London!' he snapped, throwing his hands in the air.

'I came down for the heats.'

'And I wasn't happy about it!'

'And again, last week!'

'What do you mean, last week?'

'On my own, both times.'

'Does your mother know about this?'

'No! It's got nothing to do with her. And nothing to do with you.'

'I'm your dad!'

'You didn't even notice I was gone!'

He spluttered. 'That's not the point!'

Alex made a noise of such outrage and disgust that it threw the group into silence. It was as if all the air had rushed from the room. That one sound had contained everything that needed to be said.

His father's shoulders slumped just a fraction. 'You

told me you didn't make the final,' he said.

'No, I didn't. You just assumed.'

'I found the trophy in your room this morning, when I was . . . when I didn't know where you were.' Mr Warner looked down and sighed. 'Look, mate . . . you were amazing up there. Really. You were just— And I'm sorry I missed the heat. And I'm sorry that— I'm *sorry*. I was very proud of you today, Alex. So, so proud.'

Alex gave a stare as hard as glass. 'You don't get to be proud of me,' he said. 'Not any more.' He turned to Freddie and Mr Olmos. 'Well? Are we doing this or not?'

32

'Excuse me! You're not meant to be back here.'

The three of them turned. Alex recognized the woman who'd ticked him off the register at his first heat. She had the same sour look as before. This could be trouble.

'I'm Alex Warner,' he said. 'One of the contestants.'

'Yes, Mr Warner, I recognize *you*.' She said it as if recognizing him was proof that he'd committed some terrible crime. 'The others . . . less so.'

'Oh, right,' he stumbled. 'Well, this is my . . . grandad.'

Mr Olmos's eyebrows shot up.

'Right, and who's this?' said the woman, pointing at Freddie.

'My sister,' said Alex.

She looked from one to the other doubtfully.

'Twins,' cut in Freddie. 'But from separate mothers.'

Alex jabbed her in the ribs and she gave a little gasp of pain. They could see the cogs moving in the woman's brain. Slowly. 'Well, they still can't be back here,' she said.

Mr Olmos held his palms up. 'Listen, Mrs . . . ?'

'Morris.'

'Mrs Morris.' His voice was all honey and kindness. 'This is a big day for my grandson, and he wanted to share it with us. You see, his parents were both killed recently. It's a terribly difficult time for us all. You wouldn't send us away, would you?'

Alex and Freddie stared at Mr Olmos in horror for a second and then, as one, turned their heads towards the woman. To their shock, a single tear appeared and rolled down one cheek.

'Of course,' she choked out. 'I understand.' She took Alex and Freddie's hands in her own. 'You brave, brave children,' she said.

They waited until she'd vanished around the corner.

'As if I could be a grandfather,' said Mr Olmos in disgust.

'Hang on, you're – what – three thousand years old?'

'Something like that,' he admitted, 'but I've kept very well for my age.'

It didn't take them long to find the door with Jack Kellar's name on it.

'Here we go,' said Alex, reaching for the handle. It turned easily. Not even locked. He went inside. On one side of the room was a black metal clothes rail, while opposite them a chair and table sat in front of a wide mirror that spanned the width of the wall. The rucksack was in one corner, open. An old wooden box, rougher than the one Mr Olmos had used, was clearly visible on top.

But Alex couldn't go to fetch it, because there was someone blocking the way. An enormous someone who looked at him first with surprise and then with a kind of happy malice. Kellar's bodyguard. As the ogre clambered from his seat that horrible, slow grin began to spread across his face again. But the smile didn't last long, because a second later Mr Olmos and Freddie followed Alex into the room. The bodyguard's eyes widened in fear at the sight of the old man and he stumbled backwards, tripping over the chair and ending up in a messy pile of flesh on the floor.

Freddie snorted with laughter. 'Nicely done, moron,' she smirked.

The ogre arranged his massive frame into a kneeling position and held his hands up for mercy. 'Please don't do anything to me,' he said, not taking his eyes off Mr Olmos for a second. 'You're one of *them*' – he nodded towards the bag – 'aren't you? You're one of those *things*.'

'Yes, he is,' said Alex, trying and failing to keep

his voice level.

'And if you don't do what we want then he's going to toast you like a marshmallow on a campfire,' Freddie added.

The ogre was consumed by a look of such abject misery and panic that for a moment Alex almost felt sorry for him. But then he remembered the man laughing as he had hoisted Mr Olmos into the air. Knocking him to the ground. The twisted pleasure in causing hurt.

'Give me the bag,' he said.

To their surprise the man shook his head. His breath was coming in shallow hiccups and the corners of his eyes glistened.

'Hand them over.' Mr Olmos's voice was low and rattlesnake-dangerous. 'You hand them over now.'

'You don't understand,' wailed the ogre. 'You don't know what he's like.'

'What who's like?' asked Alex.

The man looked at him as if he was mad. 'Mr Kellar,' he hissed. 'He's not . . . he's not *normal*.'

Mr Olmos took a step forward. 'You came to my house,' he said. 'You broke my things. You kidnapped me and hurt my friends. And now I'm taking them back. I don't care how much it upsets your boss.'

But instead of moving aside, Kellar's bodyguard – despite now openly sobbing – actually moved his huge bulk in front of the bag. 'You don't know what he's like,' he said again pleadingly. 'What he can do.'

'He's a stage magician,' Freddie snapped. 'He can pull bunches of flowers out of his sleeves. Big whoop. Stop being such a baby.'

'Now,' growled Mr Olmos, extending his hand, palm facing forward, 'there's something you should know.'

'What's that?' asked the ogre.

'I only had half a cup of tea this morning.'

The man's face twisted in bafflement but Alex understood.

'Brace yourself,' he whispered to Freddie.

For half a second the room seemed to warp, and everything was thrown out of focus. Alex felt an incredible pressure in his ears, as if he'd been thrust deep underwater. Then release. A pulse of white energy exploded from Mr Olmos's hand. It struck the ogre like a sledgehammer, throwing him back into the corner.

The old man took another step forward. 'You shouldn't have messed with my things,' he said, and with a flick of his hand the ogre jerked up into the air, upside down, as if he were an insect dangled by a cruel child. 'You shouldn't have taken the *jinn*,' he continued, as with another gesture he made his opponent spin in mid-air. 'And most of all,' he said as the man's face contorted into a mask of terror, 'you shouldn't have touched my friend Alex.'

He threw one arm up and the ogre was propelled like

a missile across the room, through the door and, with a sickening thud, into the wall of the corridor. He lay there, groaning and holding his head.

'Go,' Mr Olmos growled. '*Now.*'

Kellar's bodyguard glanced from him to the bag and back again. Finally, whatever terror he had of his boss came second best to the flames dancing in the old man's eyes, and he limped off down the corridor as fast as he possibly could.

Mr Olmos was breathing heavily. Alex could almost taste the magic – the perfectly controlled power – flowing from him.

Freddie let out a piercing whoop. 'That was awesome!' she screamed. 'Someone has *got* to teach me how to do that!'

Alex, though, didn't join the celebration. Something was pecking away at the back of his mind. 'It doesn't make sense,' he muttered, more to himself than the others.

'Let's just grab the bag and go,' Freddie urged.

'I mean,' Alex went on, 'why would a man like that be so scared of Kellar? It's like you said, he's just a magician.'

'Actually, I prefer the term *sorcerer*,' said a familiar, buttery voice behind them.

The three of them turned as one.

Jack Kellar stepped into the room and met Mr Olmos's gaze. At last, he seemed to find what he was looking for there because a slow smile spread across his face.

'Good to see you again, my old friend,' he said.

33

'Wonderful routine today, Alex,' Kellar went on, 'although if you're after the results then you'll have to wait like everyone else.'

'You know what we're after,' Alex said in a faltering voice. *Old friend.* What did that mean?

Mr Olmos swayed slightly on his feet. The colour had drained from his face, leaving it pale as a winter sky. 'This is Jack Kellar?' he asked.

'Of course it's Jack Kellar,' snapped Freddie. 'You must have seen him before; he's famous!'

'I never . . . You told me the name, but I never saw . . . I never thought.'

'What is it?' said Alex. 'You know each other?'

'How?' asked Mr Olmos, in a hollow, shocked voice.

'You, of course,' Kellar replied. 'I'd love to say diet and exercise, but it's *you*. You extended my life, remember?'

'But when I left you, that should all have stopped. I took that power back from you. You shouldn't be here!'

'You're right, in a way,' Kellar said. 'When you left, I was . . . *reduced*. That's probably the best word. I could barely stand. Barely eat or drink. But your magic didn't go altogether. Traces of it were left' – he pointed to his chest – 'in here.'

'Sorry to interrupt,' said Freddie, 'but what are you two talking about?'

The magician turned to her. 'Keep it a secret but I'm actually hundreds of years old.' He shrugged. 'Good trick, eh?'

'Don't be ridiculous.'

'Oh my god,' gasped Alex. All at once he could see it clearly. He understood. 'The prince. The sorcerer. *Jack Kellar* is the Sorcerer Prince.'

Freddie shook her head. 'That story you told me? But that can't be right. It's *Jack Kellar*. I mean, he's on the TV! He can't be the same man.'

'Actually, your wannabe magician friend is correct,' Kellar sneered, clapping his hands in delight. 'He told you about me then, Alex?'

'He told me you trapped him. Captured him.'

'Did he tell you what we did together? All the wonderful things we achieved?'

'He said you killed people.' Alex glanced across at Mr

Olmos, who looked as if he might topple over at any moment.

'We *built* things. Magnificent things. We built an empire together.'

'Why are you here?' Mr Olmos muttered. 'How did you know where I was?'

'Oh, I didn't!' Kellar exclaimed. 'I had no idea.' He stepped into the room and closed the door behind him. 'You see, I was in my diminished state for almost a lifetime. But at the end of it, I didn't die. I hadn't even aged. Imagine my surprise! Whatever bits of power you'd left me with were keeping me alive. So I left that place. I left our country and began to wander. Down into Africa, then up into Europe. I was the chief advisor to an emperor. I was a trader. A wise man. A musician and a writer. For a while there I was even a prophet. And eventually I came here, to England. And I thought to myself that it would be fun to do *this* for a while. A sorcerer playing at being a magician.'

He gave Alex a hard look that made his skin prickle. How hadn't he seen it before? The malice.

'The opposite of you, my boy. A trickster playing at sorcery.'

'This just keeps on getting more messed up,' said Freddie.

'Strange, I think it keeps on getting better. Of course, I always hoped I'd encounter a *jinn* again. Always told myself that one day I'd go back and claim another one.

200

I never thought for a second that one would be delivered to me, in the stalls of a London theatre! Showing off, Alex, tut-tut . . . I had my man look up the name you gave me, Mr Olmos of Hatford Cross, and then go searching. I couldn't believe my luck! But even then, I didn't suspect . . . Not until that oaf of mine came back with the three infants, prattling about an old man who burst into flames.' Kellar's face softened, becoming almost peaceful for a moment. 'Old friend,' he repeated. 'It was meant to be, don't you think? Hundreds of years and thousands of miles and here we are. You'll come back to me now, won't you? You and the three young ones. We'll be unstoppable . . .'

'Mr Olmos, will you just blast this fool already?' Freddie shouted.

'I wouldn't recommend that.'

As Kellar met his eye and winked, Alex realized what he'd been missing all along. The box at the top of the bag was empty. The thought slammed into his mind with the force of a freight train. He'd had nothing from Sally since they came into the room. Why hadn't he noticed that before? Too anxious. Too angry.

Kellar's smirk bloomed into a grin.

'Fetching, don't you think?' he asked, pulling up the sleeve of his jacket. The air was knocked from Alex's chest. There were the *jinn*, wrapped around the magician's forearm like three fire-gold bracelets. They seemed to be fused to his skin. Almost part of him.

'What have you done to them?' Alex asked. He'd meant to sound tough, but instead his words were pleading and pathetic.

'So much easier with babies like this. It took a lot more to break *him*.' He raised one finger to Mr Olmos. 'Do you want to see what they can do?'

The *jinn* flowed down his arm and into the palm of his hand, merging to form a swirling ball of flame. Alex could feel the heat, but more than that he could hear them screaming in his head. They were wild with fear, not wanting to do this man's bidding, but not strong enough to resist.

'Let them go now,' growled Mr Olmos.

'And why would I do that?'

'Because then I might let you live.'

No reply. Instead, quick as thought, Kellar sent a blast of flame rushing towards Mr Olmos.

The old man waved one hand and a concussive pulse of energy filled the room, cancelling out the attack. A bitter smell, like burnt toast.

Mr Olmos signalled again and this time a stream of perfect yellow fire poured from his hand.

Kellar countered with his own more ragged blast and the spells met in the centre of the room – two torrents of *jinn*-fire that boiled and churned against one another.

Alex felt Freddie's arm against his. Her eyes flashed with a mix of excitement and terror.

'We should help,' Alex said.

'Got any fireballs of your own handy, have you?' she responded.

The two of them turned back. The battle was no match. The sorcerer grimaced as his own attack was pushed back by Mr Olmos's greater strength. For the first time his face creased in worry and fear.

The old man still looks human, Alex thought with a shiver. What could he do in his real form?

'Stop now,' Mr Olmos commanded.

Kellar's spell weakened further but his eyes blazed with mad hate. He dropped to one knee but didn't stop sending the stream of fire. A deep groan escaped his lips. Mr Olmos took a step forward.

'All those things you made me do. All those people . . . I should have finished you when I had the chance.'

Alex expected Kellar to give up then. What else could he do? He was clearly outmatched. But instead he screwed his eyes up tight, as if he was gathering his strength. And then, with a visceral howl, he flung every last bit of magic he could rip from the *jinn* straight at his opponent. The ferocity of the blast caught Mr Olmos off guard, sending him slamming back into the wall, where he crumpled, unmoving.

'No!' screamed Alex, running across. His friend was limp as a broken doll, Freddie's face a mask of horror.

Kellar stood, hands on knees, panting hard. The smooth surface was stripped away, and only the wolf beneath remained. Teeth bared and gleaming. Eyes blood-red. Had he always been insane or had that final blast of magic pushed him over the edge? Regardless, mad he was. Wildly so.

Alex drew himself upright to face his hero, trying not to shake. He took a few paces forward, the footsteps slow and heavy. Freddie came to his side. He could hear her breathing. He swallowed and summoned his courage.

'I won't let you do this.'

'If he couldn't stop me, then how can you two?' Kellar looked almost sorry. 'How can you?'

34

'Give me them back,' Alex demanded. 'They're not yours.'

'Are they yours, then?'

'No, they're not anyone's!'

'Don't be an idiot,' Kellar spat. 'You don't have the faintest idea. This is what real power looks like.'

Alex stared. Mad orange lights danced in the man's eyes.

'It's all I ever wanted, you know,' Kellar said. 'Ever since I was your age. Ever since I realized what power really was.'

'Which is?' Freddie asked.

'Control, young lady. The means to make the world what you want it to be.'

From the corner of the room, Mr Olmos's breath came in ragged gasps.

'Being a prince was fine. People had to do as I said. But I was always searching for something else. Something different. I acquired old books, Alex. Old, even when I found them in my youth. And the things they said . . . the secrets they kept! You should have seen me then. I was a king. But I thought all that was long gone. Until you showed up. So desperate for my approval, you showed me what *you'd* found.'

Desperate. The word left razor cuts behind it.

Alex was shaking. He felt so cold. Colder than winter. Colder than death. 'You made me think that you liked me. You said you understood. You made me feel I was . . .'

'Special?' Kellar finished for him.

Alex blinked furiously. *Don't cry. Don't you dare cry.*

'You *are* special, Alex.' The sorcerer took a step towards him. 'That's why I asked to see you last week.'

'You asked all the finalists to meet you.'

'No, just you, Alex. I saw magic in you, that day you performed in the heats. Not tricks. Real magic. You don't even know you're doing it. Just small things. The way you palm a coin away from sight. For a split second it actually *does* disappear, and you don't even realize it. You crackle with magic. That's why the *jinn* responded to you. Why you could bond with them.'

Alex didn't want to hear any more. 'Give them back,'

he repeated.

'And why would I do that?'

'Because you don't deserve them. Because you're rotten inside.'

A momentary look of surprise passed over Kellar's face and then he burst out laughing.

'It really is a shame,' he said, as the mirth faded. 'I actually do like you.'

Without warning the magician threw one arm up. The three *jinn* swept into the air and burst into flame before settling beside their master.

'I wonder what Mr Donaldson would make of *this*,' Kellar said.

A wave of his hand sent a torrent of the *jinn*-fire outward. Alex and Freddie threw themselves to the floor in unison, just in time to dodge the scorching heat. The blast crashed into the wall behind, leaving it singed and steaming.

'Missed you,' Kellar taunted.

'Get out of here,' Alex hissed in Freddie's ear.

'Not without you,' she muttered.

'I'm not leaving Mr Olmos.'

'And you think I am?'

'Don't you know it's rude to whisper?' Kellar called. He was breathing hard, as if the effort of the fight was taking something out of him. The *jinn* were less bright than before. The sorcerer's lips moved soundlessly, his attention fixed on his arm, coaxing them back to life.

'What's he doing?' Freddie asked.

'No idea, but I don't think it's good,' Alex replied.

'So what's the plan?'

'I don't have a plan.'

'You should think of one. Quickly.'

Alex shrugged in exasperation.

'I mean, you can do magic mojo with the genies, right?' Freddie went on.

'Right,' Alex offered.

'So why don't you?'

'Because he's controlling them.'

'Well, you'd better sort that out then, hadn't you?'

Alex met Freddie's eyes. His heart was beating so hard it felt it would pop any moment.

'Can you do it?' she asked.

'Maybe. If you can distract him.'

'How?'

'I don't know, Fred. Just . . . just be you.'

His friend grinned. 'That,' she said, 'I can do.'

She jumped to her feet and Kellar glanced up. The *jinn* glowed more brightly once again. 'Just in time,' he said.

'For someone who's hundreds of years old you're pretty stupid, aren't you?' Freddie began.

'I beg your pardon?' Kellar had the sort of half-amused, half-baffled look on his face of someone who's just encountered an aggressive chihuahua.

'I said you're stupid. Sorry, I should have said it

louder and more clearly what with you being so incredibly old and all.'

'And why, exactly am I stupid?'

'First of all, trousers that tight don't look good on anyone over forty-five. Whatever happened to growing old gracefully? Second of all, you can't even see how great Alex is. You go on about how he's got *real magic* and don't even realize that's pretty much the least special thing about him. He's been my friend since I was basically a foetus and he's a thousand times the person you are, no matter how much you try and make him feel bad about himself. And who even does that? What kind of idiot's so insecure they get their kicks making other people feel small? Oh yeah, I know. The same kind of idiot who gets magic powers, takes over a country and then loses it all because he didn't figure that someone might, just might, want to poison his drink. That's like the most basic thing a dictator should know! You get someone else to try your food and drink first. It's obvious. Obvious! To everyone apart from you, that is. Because, as I mentioned before. You're an idiot.'

Kellar still just about had a smirk on his face, but his eyes had narrowed and his hands were balled into such tight fists that the skin of his knuckles showed white.

As Freddie ranted, Alex reached out towards Sally. Again and again he tried to connect with her, but each time his mind somehow slid off the edges. Kellar's presence was everywhere. It was as if Alex was trying to scale a sheer, slippery surface and couldn't catch hold. He concentrated. She *wanted* to come to him. And wasn't that the thing? She'd chosen him. He could feel it. See it even. She was separating from the others, drifting off to the side, as if she was sliding free of the sorcerer's gravity. *Just a little bit further*, he thought. *Just a little bit.*

'And the third thing,' Freddie went on, glancing to Alex, who gave her a small nod. 'The final reason you're stupid, Jack. The most important reason really, is this. You've been letting me go on and on and on. To prattle and rattle on just as much as I like. Which is dumb, really. Because that's given my best friend the chance to do . . . *this.*'

Alex gathered his strength and threw his mind towards Sally. There was a dizzying rush as she snapped loose from her captor and bonded with him. The violence of the moment was enough to send Kellar flying backwards into the door with enough force to crack it. He groaned, winded.

'Go!' Alex shouted. He pulled Mr Olmos up on to his feet and helped him clamber over the prone form of their fallen enemy.

Alex tried to grasp the other two *jinn* with his mind, but they were just out of reach, hovering near Kellar, not quite in thrall to him any more but still unable to break his grip. Mr Olmos had recovered enough to stumble, thank God, and the three of them made unsteady progress down the corridor, with Sally zipping around near Alex's shoulder. He could feel her there, and even in the midst of the danger pure joy thrilled through his veins.

'Stop!' came a battered voice from behind them. Alex glanced back. Kellar lurched towards them, an *ifrit* nestled in each hand. Flecks of spittle hung from his chin and his perfect suit was torn. He staggered like a boxer hit one too many times, muttering under his breath.

Another blast of fire hurtled their way and the three friends ducked around the corner just in time to see it flash past them and into the wall.

'What do we do?' gasped Freddie.

'Keep going, I suppose.'

On and on through the maze of hallways. Up and down flights of stairs until Alex had no clue what floor they were on. The theatre foyer should have been sanctuary – surely even Kellar wouldn't attack them in full view of a crowd – but they must have taken a wrong turn somewhere along the way. *Keep going. Keep going until Mr Olmos is strong enough to fight back.* With only two *jinn* left to Kellar it might just be enough.

And then they hit a dead end. A sharp turning into a short corridor with just one door that opened into a cleaning cupboard. Nothing else, and nowhere to go. Kellar stalked around the corner, licks of flame trailing from his palms, like some kind of dark angel. He was grim-faced now, the charming smile long-vanished and forgotten. This time he didn't bother to speak, to taunt or explain. He simply raised his arms and flung every bit of power he had at them.

There was nowhere to go. Nowhere to hide. No other choice for Alex but to fight back. He barely needed to think the idea before Sally had reacted, meeting Kellar's attack with their own.

Flame met flame. Strange screams seemed to issue from the roaring inferno that boiled and rumbled between them. The heat and light were intense enough that Freddie had to cower in the corner, shielding her eyes. The plastic light fittings on the ceiling melted and dripped on to the floor.

Now, at last, Alex's bravery failed him, and he closed his eyes. But he could still sense it. Still sense those ancient magics tussling for supremacy; sense every rise and fall of the battle. No, not sense. Sense is too gentle a word. He felt it inside every cell of his body. The fire came from his *jinn*, but it came from him too. And it hurt. There was a shrieking inside his head and his veins rushed with cold flame. He hung on for dear life, willing it to be over, hoping beyond hope that Kellar's power would fade first.

He didn't know how long they fought. It could have been seconds or hours. But he did notice the moment that things began to change. The moment he realized that it was them, and not Kellar, who would triumph.

Because Alex could feel the nature of the magician's power. He was *forcing* the two spirits to do his will. They were conscripts in a fight that wasn't theirs. Whereas Sally was working with him. A volunteer, who cared deeply about her side's victory. Alex understood something then about power then that Kellar did not. Power that comes from force cannot last. And cannot win out in the end.

A final push sent Kellar's last fireball hurtling back towards the sorcerer. His eyes widened in terror, and in desperation he unleashed an uncontrolled blast of energy. The explosion knocked Alex into the air. He seemed to fall in slow motion, and as he did so he saw a hole had been blasted open in the wall beside him. Through it he could see out across the stage and into the theatre's auditorium. Rows of faces stared back, making comical expressions of alarm and surprise.

As Alex hit the ground he was grateful for the darkness that took him.

35

Alex woke to find a mirror suspended above him. But no, it couldn't be a mirror. It looked like him for sure, but the face staring back had fine lines around the eyes and flecks of grey in its hair.

'Alex?' the face asked, and that wasn't his voice either. 'Oh my God, you're OK. You're alive.' And then the face was wet with tears that splashed down on to his own.

'Dad,' said Alex. His throat was raw. 'Dad,' he managed again.

His father helped him into a sitting position and then threw his arms around him. 'I thought I'd lost you,' he said, again and again.

Alex gave himself over to the embrace.

'I'm sorry, mate,' said his father. 'I'm so, so sorry for everything.'

Sirens wailed. Fire, police and ambulance. The theatre staff did their best to stop a panic, but nothing could stand in the way of the stampede towards the exits. Alex's group slowly made their way out with everyone else and then his father went off to 'find someone'. None of them were exactly sure who this someone was or what they were meant to do, but it seemed to make his dad happier.

'What happened?' Alex asked, once he was alone with his friends.

'It was so cool,' Freddie answered, her face pink with excitement. 'It was like the light got brighter and brighter and then there was this big explosion, right through the wall, and all this dust and stuff. Actually, I think it's gone up my nose. Has it gone up your nose, Mr Olmos?'

The old man looked grim, but Freddie didn't seem to notice.

'What about *them*?' Alex asked. 'When the explosion happened . . .'

Mr Olmos took something from his jacket pocket. A matchbox. He slid the white inside outward and Alex saw three objects inside, each no larger than a marble, and each glowing softly. The *ifrit*. His chest heaved with uncontrollable relief. A sob escaped. The bright autumn sun was low in the sky. They were safe. At last, they were safe.

Alex reached for Sally with his mind. *Exhaustion. Slumber. Peace.*

He leant back against a traffic bollard. It was done. 'And Kellar?' he asked.

'Vanished,' said Freddie.

'What do you mean, vanished?'

'What do you think I mean, you numpty? Like, *gone*.'

'And good riddance to bad rubbish,' added Mr Olmos.

'But he can't just be gone. He was right there. I mean, even if the explosion had – you know – then there would be, um, a body.'

'Nope,' said Freddie. 'Cool, right?'

'Then . . .' Alex tailed off. It was too awful to think of. 'I killed him?'

Mr Olmos rubbed at his wiry beard. 'No, Alex, not you. It was Kellar who sent that final attack. If he's really dead, then it was by his own hand.'

'So you think he's gone for good?'

Mr Olmos turned his face to the sky. 'Perhaps,' he said. 'To be honest, my friend, I don't know.'

Alex touched a hand to the bruise under his eye. 'What was his real name? I mean, back when . . . when you knew him.'

'It doesn't matter now. It's over now.'

Alex shuddered, but before he could reply his father

came bustling over with a confused-looking James Donaldson, Secretary of the Magic Society, in tow.

'What were you all doing back there?' the man spluttered. 'And where's Mr Kellar?'

Where *was* Jack Kellar?

It was decided by Donaldson and the other organizers that the great magician had gotten a little too big for his boots. Disappearing that way when he was meant to be judging the country's finest up-and-coming magical talent! No doubt *he* was the one responsible for the gas leak that had caused the explosion and had hightailed it before he could get in trouble. It was a disgrace, and you could be sure he wouldn't be coming back next year!

No, thought Alex, *he won't be coming back for a long time.*

In the end, the winner was a girl from Newcastle who had a mind-reading act. The trophy was presented in front of the theatre and Alex clapped just as hard as the rest of the crowd. Later, when he went to congratulate her in person, she gave him a hug. Afterwards he turned around to find Freddie looking a little bit cross for reasons he didn't quite understand.

Mr Olmos and his father were talking.

'If you ever make your own rocket,' the old man was saying, 'just make sure you follow the instructions. That was my first mistake.'

'And it exploded in your front garden? I think I read about that in the paper.'

'The local paper? Ha! Hacks! They don't know the slightest thing about rocket science!'

'Shall we get something to eat?' Freddie asked.

Rain pattered against the hard streets. Weeds sprouted here and there between the paving stones. The four of them ate pizza and then went to catch their train.

36

Someone was calling. Alex stirred beneath the sheets. He stared at the space on the wall where his Jack Kellar poster had been. The paint underneath had turned a slightly different colour, making the absence even more obvious.

'Alex, you're going to miss them if you're not careful!' came the voice from downstairs, more urgently this time.

He threw on jeans and a T-shirt, both as crumpled as each other, and flew out the front door at a run.

'Where are you going?' his dad shouted from the hall. 'I'll drive you!'

When they arrived, Agnes Taylor was already loading the car. Suitcases were flung into the boot as if they were light as pillows. Freddie stood to the side, worrying at a strand of hair with one finger, and chewing her bottom lip.

'I'm here!' Alex called, dashing across the road.

Freddie's face lit up for a brief second before she recovered herself and forced it back into an expression of boredom and indifference. Alex tried to ignore the strange things his heart seemed to be doing inside him.

'You're late,' she said.

'I overslept.'

'Five more minutes and I'd have been gone. What would you have done then?'

'I'd have called you on your phone.'

'Like that would have been the same.'

'I'm here now, aren't I?'

'Only just is the point.'

'I had to fight a powerful sorcerer, Freddie, give me a break!'

'That was two weeks ago – will you stop going on about it?'

Alex smiled. He couldn't help it. Freddie swept her hair back and up into a quick ponytail and allowed herself a quick smirk in return.

'How far is it?' he asked.

'To my aunt's? A couple of hours.'

'That's not too bad.' He glanced behind him. His dad gave a short wave. 'He said he'd drive me up whenever I wanted.'

'You're such a downer, Warner,' Freddie said, shaking her head. 'I haven't even gone yet and you're missing me already.'

'Yeah, I'm *really* missing you. I'll probably just sit and cry for days after you go.' Alex rolled his eyes.

'You probably will.'

'I definitely won't. I won't even remember what you look like tomorrow.'

'Well, your face is so average I forget what you look like when I blink.'

Alex spluttered with laughter.

'I win,' said Freddie, but her voice was low and sad.

'And there's no way your mum might change her mind?'

Freddie shook her head. 'Until next summer at least. Says the change'll do me good.'

'I'll definitely come and visit. We'll still see each other.'

'Don't do anything stupid while I'm gone, Warner.'

'I won't.'

'Like, don't get into any magical battles or whatever.'

'Do my best.'

'And don't let anyone push you around,' she added. 'That's my job.'

A breeze rippled down the street.

'Time to go now,' said Agnes Taylor.

A hard, painful ball rose in Alex's throat. He held a palm up to say goodbye and Freddie pressed hers against his.

'Bye, Alex,' she said.

He wanted to say something but found he could hardly speak.

37

There was something pinned to the door of number thirty-three. An envelope. The words 'FOR THE ANNOYING CHILD' were scribbled on the outside. Alex drew out the slip of paper it contained. One breath to steady himself before he unfolded it. Creeping worry prickled his skin.

You won't see me again, it read, *but I hope you understand that I'm doing the right thing. The only thing that can be done.*

Alex didn't bother to read any more. He hurried through the garden gate and up to the back door. It wasn't easy. Urgency made his fingers damp with sweat and he kept losing the proper grip on his lock picks. At last though, he felt the levers inside shift and the bolts slide back.

Inside was much as it had been when he'd last visited a couple of days before. Had there been anything strange about Mr Olmos then? Well, yes, of course there had. Mr Olmos was a strange man, after all. But there had been nothing out of the ordinary. Nothing beyond his usual level of bonkers. Had all that been an act?

He moved from room to room, not bothering to call out. The house was empty. It *felt* empty. Whatever life had animated it through its owner had gone. The *jinn* were gone too, Alex could sense. Unease wormed inside him.

At last he came somewhere he'd never been before – Mr Olmos's bedroom. He hesitated at the door and then pushed through.

It was almost empty. Unlike the rest of the house there was no clutter and no mess. There was a single bed, square in the centre of the room, and a few other pieces of plain furniture. On one wall was a small painting. A rough, rocky landscape at twilight. The style was the same as the one that hung in the shed. Mr Olmos must have painted this too.

He looked closer. In the centre were four figures. An *ifrit*, the size and shape of a man, and three smaller shapes around it. Lines of fire flowed from the larger creature to the smaller ones.

Alex stared. The feeling was like trying to remember

something on the tip of your tongue. He was missing something just out of reach. Just beyond him. He looked so hard and so long his eyes began to water. It was something Mr Olmos had said once. But what?

He closed his eyes and tried to take himself into that same, odd state through which he could bond with the *jinn*. It was like raising your arm or taking a step, he thought. You didn't tell each muscle and tendon to move in a certain way. You just did it.

A strange sort of calm came over him then, and when he opened his eyes he knew what it was he'd been missing. *Ascension.* That's what Mr Olmos had called it. He'd said it was almost time for the *jinn* to ascend and leave this world. The painting was the key. The painting told the story.

He felt sick and dizzy. He *had* to find his friend.

It was impossible to know where the old man had gone, but the *jinn* he'd taken with him were a different story. It took Alex no more than a few seconds to fix on their position.

The Wick.

He set off at a brisk walk, but soon broke into a jog and then a sprint. The road was wet with melted frost. Trees glowed red in the sunlight, the same colour as Freddie's hair. They flew by in a blur. Alex ran so hard it felt as if his feet were barely touching the ground.

At last he came to the entrance. The same one

through which he'd escaped Freddie and her goons. He could hardly believe it was only just over a month ago. The boy he'd been then had wanted nothing more than to be left alone with his dreams of magic. And what was he now? Something different, that was for sure. Something more complicated.

Alex bolted down the path and off into the undergrowth. Even without his connection to the *jinn* it would have been easy to find Mr Olmos – a trail had been carved through the vegetation. And all of a sudden Alex knew exactly where he'd gone.

'The Lightning Tree,' he breathed.

Mr Olmos was leaning against the blackened trunk. His eyes were closed and for a moment Alex thought he might be sleeping. The *jinn* moved in wide circles around him.

Wind rustled the leaves and numbed the tip of his nose. But was there something else there too? Another smell brought on the breeze? Baking sand and rock. Spices and salt, as potent as a breath of sea air on a still, summer day.

'I should have known,' Mr Olmos said, opening one eye. 'It's almost impossible to get rid of you, isn't it, Alex?'

'I won't let you do it.'

He smiled and pushed himself upright. 'Look at them,' he said.

They're dancing, Alex thought. There was no other

word for it. The *jinn* were performing a strange and exquisite ballet in the air. He could feel their excitement for what was about to happen. *Do they understand?* he wondered. *Do they know the sacrifice Mr Olmos is about to make?*

'I won't let you do it,' he repeated.

'How did you know?'

'The painting in your room. The large *ifrit* was you. A self-portrait. And in the picture, you were fading. Sally and the others were . . . they were taking your power. Your life. You can't.'

'And you can't stop me,' replied Mr Olmos. But though the words were harsh his voice was nothing but warm and kind. It was a simple, regrettable truth and nothing more. 'I've always known this was how it ended. This is what I've been preparing for. This is what I've been planning for.' He smiled. 'This is what I *want*.'

'Don't be an idiot!' snapped Alex. 'You don't get to want things if you're going to be this stupid.'

Mr Olmos opened his mouth to reply, but then thought better of it. Instead, he crossed the clearing and placed his hands on Alex's shoulders. His eyes were a fire that had burnt for ever. His face was a mask he wore to fit in. Alex could see the years stretching back behind this ancient, unknowable creature.

'Do you have to?' he asked.

'It's the way of it,' Mr Olmos replied. 'Young *ifrit* come into this world so rarely. They start to grow until, eventually, it's time for them to ascend. To become what they can be. What they *should* be. But they can't do it alone. They need the power of an adult *jinn* to help them on the way.'

Alex nodded. Sorrow so sharp it hurt.

'Don't be like that,' said Mr Olmos. 'It's just how it is. As natural and unchangeable as gravity. As normal as the sun rising in the morning. I am so far beyond old now. The only thing left for me to do is help them move on. That's always been my role.'

Alex felt as if the breath had been crushed from his chest. His sadness wasn't a grey thing, rather it was raw and fierce. *Like a burn*, he thought. *Just like a burn.*

'You should go,' said Mr Olmos.

Alex shook his head.

'You don't need to see this.'

'Is it . . . is it awful?' That was all he could say. His pain was too great for anything else.

'No,' the old man smiled. 'It's not awful.'

'Then let me stay.'

'Did you read the note, Alex?' he asked.

'Not all of it,' he managed.

'Well, do. And make sure to keep yourself busy. There's a lot to do, you know? Lots to learn. Lots and lots to learn. You should get yourself some hobbies.'

'I won't see you again?'

'No.'

'And them?'

'They'll go far beyond. But you never know. Perhaps one day she'll come back to you. She's chosen her real name, you know. Just now, before you came.'

'What is it?'

Mr Olmos chuckled. 'It's Sally, of course.'

Alex looked at her. His favourite. He felt her love for him and sent his own back in kind.

Clouds had come over. The sky was ice and slate. Crows circled.

And then Mr Olmos spoke. He spoke in a language that hadn't been spoken for many lifetimes of men, and never in a cold, wet, English wood. The three *jinn* came to him and their flames spread across his outstretched arms.

He was right, Alex realized. It wasn't awful at all. It wasn't fire in any way that he'd understood it before. It consumed, yes, but it was gentle and soft. It was love, in a way.

It became so that he couldn't make out where Mr Olmos ended and the *ifrit* began. They were all just a ball of burning light which grew so bright he had to turn his eyes away. And when he looked back they were gone. The Lightning Tree loomed over empty space, but the air smelt of desert sand.

Alex cried then for a while, for the friend he'd lost. And when he'd cried himself out, he walked back into the streets of Hatford Cross and opened the envelope again.

Dear Alex,

You won't see me again, but I hope you understand that I'm doing the right thing. The only thing that can be done.

I have lived for a very long time. Long enough to meet many people whom I've loved. Long enough to learn to play the flute, and to paint a few average paintings. Long enough to build things and take them apart again. Long enough to succeed many times and to fail just as often. But here, today, I am grateful that I lived long enough to meet you, my boy. You're really something.

With love,

Your Mr Olmos

Alex read the note over and over until his fingers were raw from cold. And then he went through the gates, down his drive and into his house.

His dad's head popped round the kitchen door. 'You're here!' he said. 'I wondered where you'd got to.'

'I just went for a walk.'

'Well, come on, we're going to be late.'

'Late for what?'

'For our train.'

Alex cocked his head. 'Our train?'

His dad carried two bags through with him. 'We're going away for a couple of nights. For your half-term.'

'Who is?'

'You and me.' He went on more carefully, 'If that's . . . if that's all right?'

'What about your work?'

His dad smiled. 'I'm sure they can do without me. So?'

Alex nodded his head and his father threw one of the bags his way. 'Well, I'm not carrying both of them, Alex.'

'Al's fine. If you want.'

They faced each other a moment. 'Well, come on then. Let's go.'

And together they did.

ACKNOWLEDGEMENTS

Many people have helped and supported me in writing this book.

Firstly, thanks as always to my agent, Peter Buckman, for keeping me on the straight and narrow path. Secondly to my editor, Kesia Lupo, for her immense talent and patience. To Rachel Leyshon for some brilliant ideas on how to improve the book, and for sending me a very nice email right when I was full of doubt. And of course to Barry Cunningham for his insight (and for running the whole show . . .).

Thanks also to all the rest of the Chickens – Rachel H, Laura, Jazz, Elinor, Esther, Sarah and Lucy – and, last but not least, to Helen Crawford-White for another absolute stunner of a cover design.

I'm very fortunate to have such supportive family around me. Mum, Dad and Emma, your encouragement has meant the world. And I wouldn't be doing any of this if it wasn't for the many years Ed Curtis told me that giving up was not an option.

Lastly, and as always, the biggest thanks are to my extraordinary wife, Sheba, and to my step-daughter, Isabelle. I love you both.